ROYAL

THE MYSTERIES OF THE SEPTAGRAM

PAUL BRYERS

KOBAL

THE MYSTERIES OF THE SEPTAGRAM

PAUL BRYERS

Hodder
Children's
Books

A division of Hachette Children's Books

1

The Castle on the Frozen Lake

Someone was watching her. She was alone in her room at the top of the house, lying on the floor doing her homework; it was Sunday afternoon in the middle of November, with a hint of fog in the air . . . And someone was watching her.

Or some thing. Jade shifted on to her side and looked around the room. The obvious place was the door – left slightly ajar, according to instructions. It was not unknown for her mother to creep up the stairs and peek in on her to see if she was doing what she was supposed to be doing, instead of cutting up her school books with a large pair of scissors, or piling them on top of the bed and setting fire to them, or conjuring up demons from the seventh circle of Hell or any one of the hundred and one bizarre things her mother seemed to suspect her of doing when she was alone in her bedroom.

But there was no sharp nose poking through the gap between door and lintel, not even the shadow of one on the wall.

'Mum?' she said, in case she was hovering on the landing.

No answer. Means nothing.

'Mother?' Raising her voice a little and adding accusingly: 'Are you there?'

She listened for the telltale creak of a mother creeping away down the stairs. Nothing. Nothing she could hear anyway. She surveyed the other possibilities.

Her dolls. Her *discarded* dolls. Sitting in a glassy-eyed huddle on the wicker chair in the corner. Or the menagerie of cuddly animals piled on the floor at their feet. Entirely possible that they were watching her. Resentfully. Planning revenge for the years of neglect. She should give them to a charity shop, as her mother kept telling her, instead of leaving them there to gather dust. But Jade couldn't quite bring herself to do this. Not yet.

She would if they kept staring at her, though, putting her off her maths homework. She rolled over on her stomach again and read the next question:

If one angle of a right-angled triangle is forty-five degrees, what are the other two?

Easy. 45 and 90, she wrote. Next . . . ?

How can a bear open an umbrella?

Uh?????

This question was not in 'Mathematics Key Stage 2 Test B Levels 3–5' which lay open on the floor in front of her. It was like a voice inside her head. A voice she had first heard just a few weeks ago and was becoming more and more persistent. Asking her stupid questions and telling her things she didn't want to know. Usually when she was trying to think of something else.

Bears? She had no particular interest in bears. Or umbrellas. And why would a bear *want* to open an umbrella?

It might be a bear in a circus.

Yeah, well, OK, it might.

Now go away and let me get on with my homework.

But it wouldn't go away. And now there was a picture to go with it – the image of a large brown bear holding a large red umbrella riding a unicycle – round and round in her head as if it was a circus ring

3

– and the voice was telling her in its dry but slightly mocking tones: *The claws of a brown bear are perfect for catching salmon in a waterfall or scooping honey from a hive of wild bees or ripping holes in someone's face but not for fiddling with the small metal catch on an umbrella.*

Well, thanks for telling me that, thought Jade, in the part of her brain that still seemed capable of thinking for itself, that's very interesting. I'll remember that – if I'm ever running a circus.

It could save your life.

Excuse me?

Silence.

No, go on, tell me. We don't get a lot of bears in these parts but you never know. I might run into one in the park one day on my way to school. It might be raining and it wants my umbrella.

Exactly. And you could hand it over and while it's struggling to open it, you could make your escape . . .

Where was all this coming from? It was as if there was a radio or a television programme going on in the background or she had an earpiece plugged into her mobile phone and someone kept talking to her, telling her all this rubbish.

She tried to concentrate on her homework but now she was totally distracted. Whatever the voice was, wherever it was coming from, it knew how to get her going. When she was nine she had started keeping notes on how to survive difficult or dangerous situations. Like how to survive an air crash by adopting the crash position or how to navigate by the stars if you are cast adrift in an open boat or how to light a fire by focusing the rays of the sun on to a pile of dead leaves through a piece of broken glass . . .

How to survive an encounter with a bear by giving it an umbrella might well come into this category.

But quite why she needed to know these things was a mystery, even to Jade. It wasn't as if she lived in the middle of a wilderness, like Alaska or the Mojave Desert or the Himalayas . . . or even Wales.

She lived in Turnham Green. In west London.

She climbed to her feet and walked over to the window. Her bedroom was high in the loft but it did not have a view — unless you counted the view of the houses opposite. And tonight she couldn't even see them very clearly because of the fog. She watched it climbing from the street, wiping its wet, grey rags across the windows and turning a dingy yellow in the light of the street lamps.

Turnham Green was a very quite part of London.

Once, according to her father, there had *nearly* been a battle here. Four hundred years ago during the English Civil War between the armies of the King and the Parliament. A battle that would decide the future of democracy. But it didn't happen. The two armies went away without firing a single shot.

And that, so far as Jade was concerned, just about summed up the history of Turnham Green.

She sighed and headed back to her homework.

And then she saw the screen display on her computer.

It had been changed.

Instead of the usual picture of a lighthouse with waves crashing against rocks it was of a castle on a frozen lake in the snow.

And it wasn't a still picture; the snow was actually falling.

She sat at her desk and looked at the picture more closely. It was a bit blurred and a bit dark and snowdrops kept landing on the camera and melting. As if it was a web camera showing live pictures.

Nothing unusual about this but how did it get on the screen of her computer if she hadn't put it there?

She studied it carefully. The lake was surrounded by hills and forest and the castle was at the far end on a small island with a bridge connecting it to the shore . . .

And then she saw the light. In a window, high up in the walls. Like an eye; a single, unblinking eye.

And she heard a faint sound, a sound that sent a shiver through the hairs at the back of her neck.

The distant howling of a wolf.

2

The Reindeer Herders

Something was spooking the reindeer. They rolled their eyes and tossed their heads and the old bull, Salmmo, shook his great antlers and lifted his grey muzzle to the trees and let out a long, grunting challenge with as much fear in it as defiance.

'All right, old one, easy, easy,' Tapio Turi murmured into the falling snow, as much to reassure himself as the bull, but he knew it was not all right and none of them would be at all easy until they were safely back in the village.

Old Salmmo gave another bellow. Tapio took his rifle out of its waterproof cover, pressed a cartridge into the breech and then slung it back over his shoulder. His son Aslat, who had no rifle, felt for the carved hilt of the hunting knife he wore strapped to his thigh and snapped open the little strap that kept it from falling out of the scabbard so he could pull it out in a hurry. Neither of them spoke but they shared the same grim thoughts. They were a long way from home with night falling and they had both heard the rumours. Back then, back in the village, it had been easy to laugh at them. Here, out in the forest, in the eerie Arctic twilight they did not feel quite as scornful.

They should not have been out at all so late in the year. Most of the reindeer had been rounded up almost a month ago – before the first of the snows – but a small herd had been sighted wandering along the shores of Lake Piru near the Russian border and Tapio had volunteered to go and fetch them in. There were eight cows with Old Salmmo, all but one carrying calves, and their chances of surviving the winter were not good, and not only because of the weather.

Something was stalking them, out here in the forest, something new and deadly. People said it was wolf packs, come over from Russia, but the only carcass that had been found looked as if it had been ripped apart by giant claws, much bigger than Tapio had seen on any wolf.

They were very close to the border, so close they might even have crossed back and forth without knowing. The *Sami* had never been too concerned with borders. Their ancestors had lived in this region for thousands of years before anyone had thought to call it Finland or Russia and draw lines on maps, and the reindeer wandered hundreds of miles through the forest, regardless of who owned it. Tapio reckoned they had detailed maps in their heads but they were no maps that any government would have recognized. Tapio himself was thought to be the best navigator in the village but even he wasn't too sure of his bearings so far north.

It was a relief when they came out on to the lake. At least Tapio now knew where he was. He stood on the shore and gazed out across the ice. It would be another week or two before it was thick enough to take the weight of a man, much less a reindeer, and he could still see patches of water some distance from the shore. They would just have to keep trudging through the forest. But then, as he was about to turn away, he saw the light.

'The castle,' he said.

Aslat had seen it too, and they gazed across the lake towards the ancient keep on the far shore – with the single square of light high up in one of the towers.

'So there *is* someone there,' said Tapio, who had heard the stories but not believed them until now.

The castle was the only building for miles around. It was on a small island on the north end of the lake, linked to the shore by a long stone footbridge. From a distance it looked more like a church than a fortress but it had an evil reputation. Both lake and castle were named after the *Piru*, the wicked demons of the forest, and it was believed by some that they guarded the gates of Helvata, the Nordic Hell of snow and ice.

Not surprisingly the castle was believed to be haunted and the locals gave it a wide berth – though it was in so remote an area not even the reindeer herders came near it. In recent years it had fallen into disrepair and no one knew who owned it but lately there had been a rumour that someone was living in it again. Judging from the light in the window the rumour seemed to be true.

They headed back through the trees to where they had left the herd. The animals were now close to panic. It took all the skill and patience of father and son to keep them bunched together, let alone drive them on through the forest. Finally Tapio took the rifle from his shoulder and told Aslat to stay close to the herd while he went on ahead to see if he could find what the problem was.

Not many animals could scare a full-grown bull reindeer like Salmmo. But back in the village stories were told of strange creatures that were roaming the forest. Some said they were polar bears driven far from their hunting grounds by climate change; others that they were mutants created by the radiation sickness that was in the lichens and the mosses. Either way they were large predators with a taste for reindeer. And not just reindeer. People said that two men from one of the Russian villages had failed to come back from the last round-up.

Tapio tried to put such fantasies out of his mind. Most likely the reindeer had caught the scent of a corpse, possibly another reindeer, rotting in the forest. But he tightened his grip on the rifle and kept his thumb hovering over the safely catch.

Back with the herd, young Aslat did not even have the comfort of a gun and he did not think his knife would be much use against whatever had put the fear into Old Salmmo. He peered into the depths of the forest. All he could make out was the gently falling snow and the weird and wonderful shapes it made of the young fir trees and the dead branches in the fading light – like sprites or hunched-up old witches.

He fingered the silver charm of Tuulikki, the gentle goddess of the forest. His uncle – his mother's brother, who was a shaman – had given it to him many years ago to wear on a chain around his neck as a protection against the evil ones. He was seventeen now but he still remembered the stories about the gods and goddesses of the forest; still, in his heart of hearts, believed them. Some were good, some merely mischievous, others wholly evil. And the *Piru* were the servants of the Evil One himself – Lempo, whose nickname was Paapiru, the father of demons. And so Lake Piru was the lake of demons . . .

They were just stories, Aslat told himself, but it was impossible to ignore them with the snow falling and the light fading and the wind whipping in from the Arctic and his father gone off alone with his rifle . . .

And whatever was out there, spooking the reindeer.

He wished he was safe at home in the village with his mother cooking supper and his little sister Marta prattling about something she had done at school. Or, even better, at the house of his girlfriend Liise cuddling up with her on the sofa and watching *The Simpsons* on television . . .

Salmmo let out another great bellow and turned swiftly to his right, lowering his great horns and pawing the snow with his hooves. Aslat looked past him into the trees and saw something that turned his blood colder than any wind and had him fumbling for the knife on his thigh and shouting for his father like a child.

Tapio came running back, stumbling over the roots and branches under the snow — but when he saw what had caused Aslat to cry out, his first sensation was one of relief.

It was a bear.

Only a bear.

The forests were full of them in high summer and though they could be savage at times, especially when the females had their young, for the most part they lived off berries and honey from wild bees and fish they caught in the streams and lakes. It was only if they felt very hungry or threatened that they became a menace to humans or other animals. But this bear was not a menace to anything, except perhaps itself . . . because it was caught in a trap.

It was a particular kind of trap — a cunning arrangement of logs and ropes baited with dried fish — that had been banned many years ago by the government because it condemned the animal to a lingering and painful death. The basic idea was brutally simple. The bear, attracted by the smell of the bait, put its head through a noose. As it struggled to free itself it pulled down a heavy log called the Tossing Bar. And the Tossing Bar pulled the noose even tighter around the bear's neck and forced its neck up against another heavy log called the Choke Bar, which slowly choked the life out of it.

Which was what was happening to the bear in the trap.

Tapio could tell by the glaze across the bear's eyes and the flecks of white foam round its black mouth that the process was well advanced. It was not even making a noise; it must have exhausted itself long ago, but he knew that it was impossible to free it and that even if he tried it would be in such agony and such blind rage it would turn on its rescuer – and one blow of those massive paws with the long razor-sharp claws and his brains would be spattered over the snow.

With a sigh – for it was a magnificent full-grown beast – he raised the rifle up to his shoulder and slid the safety catch. But before he could squeeze the trigger he heard something – the beginning of another bellow from Old Salmmo or a scream from his son, instantly stifled? – and he twisted round in alarm and saw the face of his worst nightmares and felt the gun plucked from his hands as if he was a child with a dangerous toy and the dark hole that was the thing's mouth opened and closed and a deep voice that was strangely distant and remote said . . . No.

'No. It is mine.'

3

Blood in the Kitchen

'It's happening,' Jade's mother said. 'I think it's time.'

She was standing in the middle of the kitchen talking on the phone.

What's happening, Jade wondered. Time for *what*?

But when she turned round and saw Jade watching her she looked embarrassed and said, 'Can't talk now, ring you back.'

She clipped the phone back on its base, picked up a knife and started chopping raw onions. She might as well have started whistling, it wouldn't have been any less suspicious.

'Who was that?' asked Jade.

'None of your business,' said her mother. Then, after a moment: 'Someone from work.'

She peered through her glasses at the cookery book propped on the kitchen unit.

'Have you been messing with my screen display?' Jade demanded.

'What screen display?'

'The screen display on my computer.'

'No. Why should I?'

'I don't know but someone has.'

'It was probably you and you forgot.'

She scraped the bits of onion into a bowl and started chopping up carrots. Jade watched her with rising irritation.

I bet it *was* her, she thought.

But why would her mother *want* to change her screen display?

She didn't have an answer to that and you better believe she wasn't going to get one from her mother.

She wandered over to the window, pressed her face up against the glass to cut down on the reflections and peered gloomily out at the back yard. Not that you could see much in the fog. Just the shed where they kept their bikes and the top of the neighbour's fence and a bit of tree against the darkening sky.

'I hate November,' she said.

Her mother kept chopping.

'Nothing ever happens in November. It's just a nothing time between Hallowe'en and Christmas. And then it's January.'

'Haven't you got homework to do?'

'Finished it.'

'You don't seem to be spending very long on it these days.'

Jade shrugged.

'Are you finding it too easy?'

Another shrug.

'Well, if you've got nothing better to do you can lay the table.'

'Have we always lived in Turnham Green?'

The chopping stopped. Jade turned round. Her mother was staring at her with the knife in her hand. *Like a witch cutting up babies.*

What had put that in her head? Her mother looked a bit like a witch — she was tall and thin with a sharp nose and long hair that was often all tangled up and she couldn't do anything with and was turning grey already — but cutting up babies? Gross.

'What's the matter?' she said.

'Why do you ask that?' said her mother.

'I just wondered, that's all. I just wondered if we'd ever lived anywhere else.'

19

'No.' Sharply. Then, after a small pause: 'Not since you were born.'

'So I was born in Turnham Green.'

'Yes. Well, not exactly.'

'So where *was* I born?'

Another small pause. Then: 'Berkshire.'

She started chopping again, even more furiously than before.

'Berkshire?'

Jade tried to place Berkshire on a map of England. It was one of the counties just to the west of London, she thought.

'Where in Berkshire?'

'Does it matter?'

'Yes. I want to know where I was born.'

'Rackthorne,' said her mother, after another long pause. It was like getting blood out of a stone.

'Rackthorne?' Jade had never heard of it. 'What's Rackthorne?'

'It's a village in Berkshire. Now will you let me get on with cooking supper. Before your father gets home.'

'Why were you living there?'

''Cos we were.' Chop chop . . .

'And how old was I when we moved?'

'Two.' Chop. Knife paused. Thinking about it. 'No. Less.'

Chop, chop.

Jade watched her for a moment. Then she said: 'Didn't you ever want any other children?'

Her mother gave a sudden yelp and dropped the knife.

'Now look what you've made me do.'

She stood there dripping blood from her finger. Jade ran to the drawer with the plaster.

'Let's see,' she said.

It wasn't much of a cut. You'd think from the fuss she was making she'd sliced half her finger off.

'Run it under the tap,' she said.

'I feel faint.'

Her mother couldn't stand the sight of blood.

Jade took her by the hand and led her over to the kitchen sink to run her finger under the cold water tap. She watched the blood drain away with the water.

'Now hold it up,' she said. 'So the blood doesn't run into it.'

Her mother held her finger up, looking away with her eyes all scrunched up.

Jade took the plaster out of its wrapper and then

pulled her mother's arm down so she could reach but with the finger still sticking up like a rude gesture. She dried it with kitchen roll and wrapped the plaster round it.

'It'll be all right,' she said. And then because she felt a twinge of guilt, 'Do you want me to finish chopping the carrots?'

'Please. I think I'll have to sit down for a minute.'

So Jade led her into the sitting room and sat her down on the sofa, telling her to keep holding her finger in the air. Then she went back into the kitchen to chop carrots and despite her remorse she couldn't help thinking that her mother had picked a very convenient time to start chopping her fingers off, just when they were starting to talk about something interesting.

'What else do you want me to do?' she shouted when she'd finished.

'Just lay the table,' said her mother faintly.

Jade yanked open the drawer where they kept the cutlery and then she saw the knife where her mother had dropped it on the floor. There was a smear of blood on the blade. She picked it up and wiped it clean with the kitchen roll. At least it was red like any normal person's.

'Have you ever wondered if your parents are like –
aliens?' Her friend Miriam had asked her once after a
short stay in Jade's house.

The answer was a rather curt No and an enquiry
as to whether Miriam ever wondered if her parents
were like – *Muppets*?

Jade did not wonder if her parents were aliens, not
seriously, but she did sometimes wonder –
increasingly of late – who they *were*.

Perhaps this wasn't so strange. Lots of people
didn't know who their parents were. They were
either Old Parents or Young Parents. Happy or
Sad. In a Good Mood or a Bad Mood. Married
or Divorced. They had jobs or they didn't have
jobs. And if they had jobs, they were either jobs that
you knew something about – like teachers or taxi
drivers or doctors or dinner ladies or traffic wardens
– or jobs you knew little or nothing about, like
financial advisers or stock market analysts or
pharmaceutical consultants . . .

For a while, when she was a little kid, Jade had
thought her father was a burglar.

That's what he had told her. He said he was a cat
burglar. At the time Jade thought this meant a man
who stole cats but she soon gathered that it meant a

man who stole from houses by climbing up walls and through windows – like a cat.

Amazingly, she had believed him. She was embarrassed about this now because although her father looked a bit like a cat – a fat, ginger one – he didn't look anything like a cat burglar. You could imagine him curled up by the fire but you couldn't imagine him climbing walls or squeezing through windows. He was short and tubby with thin ginger hair and a small ginger moustache. He looked utterly respectable. And yet when she was little Jade used to feel quite anxious when she was out with him in case he broke into a house and left her outside to keep watch. Or even worse, took her in with him. Once he had taken her on a visit to a stately home and announced his intention of 'Sussing Out The Joint' in case he had to 'Do A Job There'. She had been seriously alarmed, but that was the only time it had really bothered her and some time later she had realized he was having her on and his real job was nowhere nearly as interesting or as dangerous as being a cat burglar. And a little after that she had come to the conclusion that he had made it up to impress her, to make her think he was more interesting than he really was.

His real job was being a civil servant. He worked in the Home Office checking people's passport applications. And her mother worked at home marking exam papers.

And that was one of the very few things that she knew about them.

Oh, she knew what they were like to live with. Their likes and dislikes and stuff like that. They were both quite old-fashioned and set in their ways. They didn't like bad language or reality television. Her father had a weird sense of humour and an irritating habit of humming to himself when he was pottering around the house. Her mother couldn't stand the sight of blood . . .

And despite the fact that she spent most of her time marking exam papers she never seemed to be able to give you a straight answer to a straight question.

But that was about as far as it went . . .

Part of the problem was that neither of them had a family of their own, people who told you where they were coming from and what they were like when they were younger. Her father's parents had been killed in a car crash when he was a child and he'd brought brought up by grandparents who died when he was in his early twenties, before Jade was born. And Jade's mother didn't even know who her parents were. She'd been brought up in a convent and then by a series of foster parents.

Neither of them ever talked about their own childhood, except to say that it hadn't been much fun. There was no home town they went back to, no childhood friends, no streets where they had grown up, no schools they pointed out to her where they had spent the first few years of their lives. In fact it was hard to imagine either of them *as* children. It was as if they had come to earth as grown-ups – to be her parents.

'Oh, Jade, how *could* you?'

Her mother was standing in the door, looking pale, with her finger still stuck up in the air and a sad, people-always-let-me-down look on her face. Like a religious statue pointing towards heaven. Except that the plaster rather spoiled the effect.

'How could I what?' said Jade.

'Lay the table without wiping down the surface,' said her mother.

'It doesn't need wiping,' said Jade, looking at it. It was spotless.

But her mother sighed heavily and limped over to the kitchen sink for a cloth.

Why does a cut finger make you limp, Jade wondered?

But she took the cloth off her and moved all the cutlery and wiped the table that didn't need wiping and then set out the cutlery again and then went back up to her room in the loft because all things considered she was better off out of the way.

And besides she wanted to see what had happened to the screen display on her computer.

At first she thought it had gone because the screen just looked blank.

But then she saw that it wasn't blank. It was dark. And if she stared at it carefully she could see the falling snow against the sky and the tiny light glowing in the distance . . .

4

Be He 'Live or Be He Dead

The priest sat in his darkened study and watched the snow swirling in the floodlights in front of the church. The church was usually only lit up on saints days and feast days – and only for the most important saints and feasts at that – but tonight the priest had switched the floodlights on. So that a stranger driving north could see it through the dark and the snow . . .

It was almost ten o'clock and the priest had been watching from the upstairs window for twenty minutes – ever since he took the phone call. He did not know why he was sitting up here in the dark – he could have waited more comfortably in the sitting room by the fire – but he did not have much else to do and it felt more correct, somehow, to keep a vigil, rather than slump in front of the television, as he usually did in the evenings.

He saw the headlights of a car coming from the direction of town and leaned forward in anticipation, but it swept past in a spray of snow and slush and he watched the tail lights disappearing into the dark. There was not much traffic at the best of times and on a night like this few people would travel unless they really had to. And yet his visitor had chosen to drive three hundred kilometres in the darkness and the snow, after the long flight from Rome. He must be very anxious to get here. Or else eager to do what had to be done and head back south as soon as possible.

Another car.

And this time it slowed as it approached the church – the priest's glowing beacon in the dark – and turned into the narrow drive.

The priest hurried downstairs and opened the door, bracing himself against the cold and blinking in the snow and the glare of the headlights as the car swept across the front of the church and came to a halt outside the presbytery. The driver switched off the engine and the lights dipped and dimmed. Silence and the softly falling snow. Steam rising from the bonnet of the car. And then suddenly it wasn't a car any more.

It was a horse.

A magnificent war horse – a knight's charger – with its head and most of its body draped in a black caparison decorated with a white cross, stamping the frozen ground and blowing steam from its nostrils.

And it had a rider. A knight wearing a long black robe over his armour with the same white cross on chest and shoulder who turned towards him . . .

The priest staggered as if he had been struck. He was about to fall on his knees thinking it was the Angel of Death, come for him at last. But then through the falling snow he saw that it was a car again – a black 4 x 4 Audi with ski racks on the top – and the driver was climbing out and striding stiffly towards him; a tall figure in jeans and a hooded jacket, smiling and stretching out a hand . . .

'Father Johann?'

For a moment the priest could only stare as if at a ghost and although the stranger stayed smiling, the smile was accompanied by a puzzled frown as he stood there in the doorway, half in and half out of the snow.

'I am sorry.' The priest passed a hand over his

brow and made an attempt to pull himself together. 'I am sorry. I feel a little . . . The sudden cold, I think . . .'

'You must go inside at once,' said his visitor, all concerned, physically pushing him backwards through the door and following, pulling it shut behind him. 'Why don't you sit down?' the door to the sitting room was open and they could see the log fire in the hearth. Father Johann allowed himself to be manoeuvred through the door and into an armchair.

He felt a little better now. It must have been an illusion. A hallucination. The difference in temperature, the snow and the lights playing tricks with his eyes or his mind . . . His eyes were failing and sometimes if he had been reading or working on the computer it took them a while to readjust to greater distances. And sometimes he felt giddy if he stood up too quickly but . . . he had never seen a car change into a horse before. He smiled at his foolishness.

'Forgive me,' he said again. 'It is not how I meant to welcome you. It is Brother Benedict, yes?'

He tried to stand up but the man held him by his shoulder so he had to remain seated. A gentle but powerful grip.

'Benedict,' he said. 'Please, sit for a moment, and if you will permit I will fetch in my things.'

'But I must help you . . .'

'I have very little and I won't be a moment.'

And then he was gone.

The priest was annoyed with himself now. He was not an old man, barely sixty, and in what his friends considered to be rude health and he felt as if he had made the wrong impression. He stood up − to reassert himself as much as anything − and threw another log on the fire, though it did not need it. Then he stood leaning on the mantelpiece to await the return of his visitor.

He was back in less than a minute toting a rucksack and a pair of skis wrapped in a plastic cover.

'Where may I . . . ?'

'Oh just leave them in the hall for now. I'll show you your room in a minute. But come, *you* must sit − you've had a long drive . . . and a long journey from Rome . . .' The priest was his old self now, anxious to be hospitable. 'You left this morning, I gather.'

Benedict came into the room and sat close to the fire warming his hands by the blaze. He was a young man by the priest's standards: in his early thirties perhaps – younger than he had sounded on the phone – with fresh open features and short blond hair. He wore a T-shirt under the hooded sweater with some sort of logo on it. The Angel of Death, the priest thought scornfully, smiling at himself now . . . He felt like he'd had a new lease of life and rubbed his hands together, like the host of an inn.

'You will have some supper? My housekeeper has left something on the stove for us.'

They had been most insistent – the people in Rome – that he should be alone when he met the reverend brother. It was necessary to be discreet, they said.

'You are vegetarian, I was told. Yes, well we have a good vegetable soup . . .' They could smell it simmering in the kitchen. 'But first a drink. You *do* drink?' He had a moment's doubt. 'Perhaps . . .' He wished now he had read more about the Order.

'Thank you. I do drink.' His smile crinkled his eyes. Eyes that seemed much older than his face, somehow; they studied the priest with dry amusement as if he found him a curiosity, a rarity . . .

And so I am, thought the priest, a Catholic priest in a country that is overwhelmingly Protestant with a parish that covers thousands of square miles of snow and ice and forest . . . and with fewer than a dozen regular churchgoers.

'Something strong and warming,' he proposed. 'I have vodka or schnapps – or a glass of red wine?'

'Wine would be perfect, thank you.'

The priest took a bottle out of the rack in the kitchen and poured for them both, though he personally would have preferred vodka.

'Here you are,' he said. 'A Pinot Noir, good for the heart. But not Finnish of course. The grape will not grow so far north – you may find that no surprise . . .' He was babbling a little, betraying his nervousness. They were speaking English, as they had on the phone. Father Johann had spent several years in England, as a teacher, and spoke the language well. But now he raised his glass and gave the Finnish toast: 'Kippis!'

'Cheers.' The visitor drank, regarding the priest with that same dry amusement across the top of his glass. Then he said. 'You are Swedish, I believe.'

'Correct. But I have been living here in Finland for many years. And here in the far north, I think, there is little difference between us, Finn, Swede or Norwegian, we are all the same. Norseman, all. And you, Brother?'

He could have been a Norseman, too, with that colouring: a Viking with eyes like the northern seas that changed with the light from blue to grey.

'Me? I am English.'

The priest was surprised, though his English was, in fact, perfect.

'I had thought it was a Germanic Order, exclusively.'

'Not at all. Well, it was, once upon a time. But now there are many nationalities. Though I believe I am the only Englishman.'

'I confess I didn't know it still existed,' Father Johann said. 'The Order, I mean. I had to look it up on the Internet.'

'Oh, yes. We still exist.' That smile again, as if recalling a private joke. 'Though not as many as we once were or as powerful . . . or militant.'

A warrior monk, thought the priest, in this day and age. In my sitting room. He shook his head as an image of the horse and its ghostly rider flickered briefly across his mind.

'But let's eat,' he said. 'And I'll tell you what you've come so far to hear.'

They had a thick vegetable soup with bits of pasta

floating in it – probably because the housekeeper knew the visitor came from Italy (the priest had not been *that* discreet) – which they ate with a black rye bread, sour and grainy, washed down with more of the wine.

The visitor raised his glass, studying the dark-red liquid in the light.

'If you are not too tired,' he said, 'I would very much like to hear your account of these mysteries you have witnessed.'

'Mysteries,' the priest repeated, nodding as if he approved the term. 'Yes, they are that – though I have not witnessed them myself, not at first hand. But first let me ask you: what do you know of the *Sami*?'

'They are the reindeer herders, yes? The Lapps?'

'Yes, though they would not thank you for calling them that. It's not a name they call themselves. They are a very old, very proud race, the *Sami* – the original hunter gatherers who were here long before the Finns, or the Swedes or the Russians . . .'

'I'm sorry. I know little of them.'

'Few people do. They were persecuted for centuries. Forbidden to speak their language, practise their religion, even use their own names, their *Sami* names, that is. They were considered to be pagans,

Devil worshippers. Children of Satan. But the *Sami* survived. Somehow they kept their traditions alive – in secret. And now they are tolerated and there are laws protecting their culture. Though there's not very many of them, of course. I think fewer than five thousand in a population of five million. And yes, most of them are reindeer herders.'

'Tell me about that.'

'The reindeer? Well, there's not much to tell. The *Sami* used to hunt them in the old days. Then they started to keep herds. They keep them on farms in the winter and then in the spring and the summer they let them out to wander through the forest. They head for the highlands – the fells – to escape the mosquitoes. And some of them roam for miles – hundreds of miles – but always to the same area. They seem to have some kind of map in their head that tells them how to get around. Then in the autumn they're rounded up and brought back to the farms for counting – and calving . . . and slaughter. Have you ever eaten reindeer meat?' A shake of the head. 'But of course, you're a vegetarian. Well, it's very good, very popular – in Scandinavia at least. The reindeer are vegetarians, too. All they eat are mushrooms and moss and berries and lichen . . . About a hundred and fifty different plants, someone told me. That's what makes the meat taste so good. But, what was I saying . . . ?'

'The round-up.'

'Ah yes. The round-up. Well, it must have been about a month ago they started bringing them in, before the worst of the snows – and that's when the rumours started. They found a lot of carcasses. Badly mutilated.'

'Mutilated? In what way? Did they describe it to you?'

'I saw for myself. One of them. they took me into the forest to show me. They . . . I think they wanted someone outside their own . . . society . . . to confirm their suspicions.'

'Which were?'

'That it was something . . . supernatural.'

'And did you?'

The priest did not reply directly.

'I have never seen anything like it,' he said. His face had lost its ruddy glow and had an unhealthy pallor in the light. 'I cannot imagine what animal could have done that. Unless it was a sabre-toothed tiger.' He smiled as if it was a joke but it was not a very convincing smile and the eyes he raised to the monk's were troubled. 'Or a man with a very wicked knife. And that was the other thing – it hadn't been eaten.'

'Perhaps it was disturbed – whatever it was that killed them.'

'Perhaps. But others that were killed were butchered – cleanly – most of the flesh removed and the rest – *arranged*. Skull and horns, skin . . . entrails. Like . . . a warning. Like primitive tribes left in the past – to mark their territory – to warn others to stay away.'

The monk nodded to himself as if this made perfect sense, or fitted with some other things he knew.

'And the men? You said in your report that some men have gone missing from the villages.'

'Yes. The rumours started a few weeks back. That a couple of herders had gone missing during the round-ups. But it was from a village on the Russian side of the border so no one knew if it was true or not – there's a degree of lawlessness on the Russian side – but two weeks ago two people, a man and his son, went missing from one of the Finnish villages. And that's when I made my report.'

'What about the police – the authorities? Have you spoken to them? Are they involved?'

The priest seemed to brood a little. 'They know but . . .' He shrugged . . . 'They are not involved, as far as I am aware.'

'Why not?'

The priest needed to think about this for a moment. Then he said: 'The authorities have come to accept the *Sami* as a race apart. They no longer try to make them, what is the word . . . to be like them . . . *assimilate*. They leave them to their own ways, their own customs and beliefs – but . . .' He spread his arms. 'They think they are like children who believe in ghosts – witches and warlocks, trolls and goblins, strange, supernatural beings of the forest. Like you English think of the Celts and the Irish. Full of superstitions, their heads full of myths. They take them with, what is the expression? A pinch of salt.'

'And you do not?'

'Oh – they are full of stories, the *Sami*, about the wild things of the forest. Not just the bears and the wolves but . . . other things. The *haltia* – I don't know if there is an exact translation – gnomes or sprites, elves perhaps. Spirits who dwell in particular parts of the forest, some among the trees, some in the lakes, some in the air . . . Some good, some bad.

And *piru*, much more dangerous creatures, evil creatures, demons . . .

'The *Sami* will tell you the stories but I don't know if they believe them – any more than we believe in our own folk tales. Do you believe in Little Red Riding Hood? Or perhaps the English do not have fairy tales, I cannot remember. But they do, I remember now, even the English who are so rational. There is the Green Man, is it not, the ancient god of the forest, Puck, Robin Goodfellow . . . ?'

'I believe they do not go in for mutilating reindeer, not in England.'

'No. No, they wouldn't. Well, there you are. That is all I can tell you I think.'

'There was something about a castle on a lake.'

'Ah yes. The castle on the lake. Castle Piru. Named after the demons. Well, I do not know if there is a connection, there is no evidence of one but . . . there is a belief locally that the castle is haunted – no one has lived in it for years, it was practically a ruin, a refuge for bats and owls and . . . other creatures.'

'You say *was*. It *was* a ruin?'

'Yes. There was some work done there a year or so ago, some renovation work and . . . lately there have been reports of lights at night, signs of . . . residence.

And I suppose you could say that these ... incidents ... have occurred in the vicinity of the castle. So, naturally, some of the *Sami* are inclined to make a connection. The castle has had a bad history.'

'How far is it from here?'

'Oh, not far. Not as distances are measured in these parts. Thirty, thirty-five miles to the north-east, on the Russian border. In fact, that is the problem, really, when it comes to finding out what is going on there because it may, in fact, be *over* the border.' He saw that his visitor was looking confused. 'The border goes right through Lake Piru. The castle is on an island in the lake, some say it is in Finland, some in Russia. You could say it was a kind of No Man's Land. Finland was as you know for many years a part of Russia, a Grand Duchy under the Tsars. It became independent as late as the twentieth century and since then, in living memory, there have been two wars with Russia. Even now the question of the border has not been entirely settled to everyone's liking. And I do not think the Russians are much in control of what happens on their side of it. There is much smuggling. Banditry. Armed gangs. We call it the Badlands.'

'How can I get there? Is there a road?'

'You want to go there?'

The smile again.

'As I have come so far.'

'Forgive me for asking but . . . what is your interest in this matter, precisely?'

'I regret I cannot tell you that. I am sorry if you feel I am being discourteous but I am under a vow of secrecy – to my superiors.'

Father Johann bowed his head in acceptance of this and kept his thoughts to himself.

He sighed. 'Well, there is not a road as such. A track, maybe. Through the forest. You would need a guide.'

'Could you . . . ?'

But the priest shook his head. 'I don't know my way around the forest. You'd need one of the *Sami* to take you. I can put you in touch with someone. A man called Jussa.' He smiled. 'My own name in *Sami*. Johann, or Johannes. And he too is a priest. Of a kind. What is the English word – a man of magic, a wizard . . .'

'A shaman?'

'A shaman. Yes. I suppose you might call him a shaman.'

'I will be very interested to meet him.'

'I will ring him in the morning. It is a little late now.'

'I appreciate this,' said his guest. 'And I am sorry I cannot be entirely frank with you.'

The priest shrugged. 'You do what you have to do. Like all of us in the service of the Church. And now I expect you would like to see your room.'

He stood up and led his visitor out into the hall. Brother Benedict picked up his luggage.

'You can leave the skis there,' said Father Johann. 'They're not in the way.'

'I'll take them up if you don't mind,' said his guest after a slight hesitation. 'I need to check the bindings.'

The priest was surprised. He would have thought it could keep until morning but he said nothing and led the way up the stairs.

He would have been even more surprised if he had seen what the monk did when he was left alone in the privacy of his room.

First he took the skis out of the plastic cover and laid them flat on the bed. Then he took a small screwdriver, unscrewed the metal bindings that the ski boots were meant to fit into, and screwed them together to form a single mechanism about a metre long with a hole at one end.

Next he took one of the ski poles and pulled off the rubber grip to expose a hollow metal tube, or barrel, which slotted neatly into the hole. Then he took what looked like a metal crucifix from his bag and fitted it into a slot at the bottom of the mechanism.

Had the priest seen the object now lying on his bed he would have been puzzled to explain its purpose for either skiing or religion. Indeed, even he might have spotted the resemblance to a modern automatic rifle.

Benedict pressed a hidden catch in the 'crucifix' to release a metal bar that served as the trigger. Then he delved in his backpack again and took out a camera bag containing a Fuji S7000 digital camera. Inside one of the compartments, wrapped in a yellow duster, was a long plastic object which a security check might take to be a zoom lens but which was, in fact, a 10 x 40mm telescopic sight, much favoured by hunters – or snipers. And the ten spare 'batteries' in the camera bag were 15mm-calibre bullets; bullets that shone with a silvery gleam even in the poor light of the bedside lamp. Finally he prised open the base of the crucifix to reveal a spring-loaded rifle magazine, loaded it with five rounds of the silver bullets and put the others in the pocket of his jacket.

Then he put the rifle and the skis back in the ski bag, zipped it up, cleaned his teeth and went to bed.

Father Johann meanwhile was saying his prayers. When he had finished and climbed into bed he found he could not sleep. He was worried about the reindeer herders; he was worried about what was happening to the reindeer; he was worried about what was *making* it happen; but most of all he was worried about his visitor from Rome.

Why had he come all the way from Italy because of a few missing reindeer herders and a few mutilated reindeer?

There was something strange about all of this. Stranger even than Father Johann had thought when he first heard the stories from the shaman Jussa Proksi. He wondered if it had been such a good idea to mention Jussa to his visitor. But Brother Benedict came with glowing references from the highest offices of the Church. Father Johann had been told by his bishop to give him every assistance.

Even so . . .

He wished he knew more about him — and his mysterious Order.

An Englishman, too.

Fee! Fie! Foe! Fum! I smell the blood of an Englishman. Be he 'live, or be he dead, I'll grind his bones to make my bread.

The old nursery rhyme came to the priest's head unbidden, surprising him after so many years. When was it he had heard it last? When he was teaching in England, back in the seventies, a young priest in a Catholic school in Lancashire, and the children singing it in the playground; he could hear them now, a distant echo . . .

He couldn't sleep.

He made himself get up, thinking he might make himself a hot drink but he found himself pausing outside the guest bedroom. There was no light coming from under the door, no sound from within.

Then, almost without thinking, he wandered into his study and closed the door firmly behind him and switched on the computer.

He tapped the name of the Order into Google.

There were several pages of references. Last time he had just looked it up on the Catholic Encyclopaedia but now he tried a couple of the others just in case they told him something different.

But on the whole the facts were the same. The Order had been founded in Jerusalem at the end of the twelfth century – one of the several orders of crusader knights. When they were driven out of the Holy Land they were employed by the King of Hungary to fight the pagans on his eastern borders. They carved out a homeland for themselves in the land now known as Transylvania on the shores of the Black Sea but after some obscure scandal involving their leader, or Grand Master, they moved again to northern Europe. For hundreds of years they had slaughtered or enslaved many they considered to be the enemies of the Church – until the Church itself decided they had gone too far in their zeal for converts and conquest and attempted to rein them in.

Father Johann already knew something of this but as a part of Church history and not the most attractive part – though the brothers of the Order had done much to redeem themselves in later years. They were a simple religious order now but they still seemed to Father Johann like a relic of the Middle Ages – though Brother Benedict seemed modern enough.

On a whim he decided to type the monk's name

into Google to see if it came up with anything. But what *was* his name? His full name. He had it somewhere, in an email. Ah, here it was. Benedict Ullman. No wonder the priest had not thought of him as English. Austrian, he had thought, or a Germanic family from northern Italy. He tapped it into the search engine, not really expecting to find anything.

But he did. Not much – but enough to send a shock, like a splinter of ice, into his heart.

Benedict Ullman, he read. Knight of the Order of St Saviour of Antioch. Born Transylvania 1225.

A coincidence, surely, or a mistake. But there was no other of that name. And he had a sudden fearful image of the ghostly figure turning toward him in his long black robe with the white cross of the Order on his shoulder and chest and the war horse stamping and steaming in the drifting snow . . .

5

Miss Simpson Goes Bats

The first thing Jade did when she woke up in the morning was check out the screen display on her computer.

It was back to normal.

No castle, no lake, no snow. Just the usual image of the lighthouse and the sea breaking over the rocks.

'Jade.' Her mother calling up the stairs. 'Are you up yet?'

Jade sighed, switched off the computer and prepared for another average day in Turnham Green.

She washed her face, got dressed and went downstairs for breakfast. The morning news was on the radio; her father was getting his things ready for work; her mother was making sandwiches for their packed lunches.

Jade poured herself a glass of orange juice and a bowl of cereal and sat down at the kitchen table.

'In the bathroom,' she said.

She took a mouthful of cereal. The man on the radio said that Hurricane Sadie was fast approaching the Florida coastline. The clock on the kitchen cupboard moved another second closer to eight o'clock.

Then she realized they were both staring at her.

'What?' she said.

'What did you just say?' said her mother.

'I said it's in the bathroom.'

'What's in the bathroom?'

'Dad's watch.' She jerked her head in his general direction.

'Why did you say that?' said her father curiously.

'Because you just said, "Where's my watch?"' suggested Jade.

'No, I didn't.'

'Yes, you did.'

'No, he didn't.'

Jade considered. Were they both mad or was she? She had distinctly heard him say, 'Where's my watch?'

Or had she?

Well, someone had said it.

Her mother pursed her lips and went back to making sandwiches. Her father nodded slowly to himself a few times and then went upstairs and came down half a minute later with his watch on his wrist. He and her mother exchanged meaningful glances.

And Jade wondered if she'd get a migraine again.

She always got a migraine when she heard voices. Almost always anyway.

They had started a few weeks ago; the voices *and* the migraines.

Sometimes there was just one voice and sometimes there were lots of them. It was as if she was listening to a radio in her head but a radio that wasn't tuned in properly. Or searching through different wavebands. You'd catch the odd word and then there'd be stuff in a foreign language or just loads of crackle and static. And then sometimes she'd hear one complete sentence loud and clear.

Like *Where's my watch?* or *How does a bear open an umbrella?*

The migraines were something else. They seemed to come in different shapes and sizes and she only knew they were migraines because she'd described them to her mother who'd said that's what they sounded like and if they got any worse they'd have to go to the doctor and get a prescription for them.

Jade couldn't imagine how they could get any worse. They started off with a feeling of not really being there; and her head felt as if it was full of treacle, except that it was thicker and more solid than treacle, more like marzipan. And all the sounds she heard were filtered through it so as if they were muffled or came from a great distance. And sometimes it affected her vision. It felt as if part of her eye had been blanked out. Just a small part, slightly to one side, so that whatever she was looking at there was a bit missing, like a piece of a jigsaw puzzle that had been left out.

And then the snake came. A writhing snake with a diamond pattern on its back, moving across her eye from right to left. And then starting from the right again. And after the snake came the headache. So bad she wanted to throw up. Or just lie down in a dark room until it went away.

But she didn't seem to be getting a migraine now. She moved her head experimentally from side to side just to see if it was lurking about somewhere.

'Now what are you doing?' said her mother.

'Nothing,' said Jade.

'Well, hurry up or you'll be late for school.'

'Jade.'

'Miss?'

'What did I just say?'

Jade thought about it. *Had* she just said something?

'Sorry, miss,' she said.

She hadn't been listening to Miss Simpson; she'd been thinking about the voices in her head and wondering where they came from. The incident of the watch was an important clue. Because clearly that particular voice – the voice that said *Where's my watch?* – had come from inside her father's head.

So did that mean she could read her father's mind?

And were all the other voices coming from her father's head?

She sincerely hoped not.

'I said, can anyone tell me the difference between a producer and a consumer?'

Jade saw that a number of people had their hands up. Some of them were saying, 'Miss, miss,' like they were just bursting to tell her.

'A producer makes its own food – like a lettuce –

and a consumer eats it like . . . like a caterpillar,' suggested Jade.

Miss Simpson stared at her with active dislike. Jade was not Miss Simpson's favourite pupil. They rubbed each other up the wrong way. Jade's friends called Jade 'Miss Simpson's Pet' because she so obviously wasn't.

'I do not recall asking you for an answer,' she said. 'I asked you what I had just *said*. If you think you have the right answer what do you do?'

'Put my hand up and wait to be asked.'

Miss Simpson thought that Jade was too clever by half. But that was no reason for picking on her all the time. Or talking to her as if she was aged six.

'Right – now we've got that straight . . . Producers make their own food and consumers eat them. Plants are the Producers. Animals are the Consumers.' She wrote it on the blackboard so they would all remember. Then turned back to face the class. 'Now, who can name me the links in a typical food chain?'

The hands shot up again. Not Jade's. She was bored. She quite liked science when they did experiments but not when Miss Simpson was talking at them all the time. She was a large woman with a loud voice. She had a mass of red hair that she wore piled on top of her head with wispy strands that hung down around her face and made her look a bit mad. And she wore large round spectacles that magnified her eyes and made her look even madder. Mad and scary. Even the loudest, mouthiest kids in class were a bit scared of Miss Simpson. Even some of the other teachers. You never knew quite what she was going to do next.

'Cabbage, slug, thrush, hawk,' she repeated as she wrote them down on the blackboard. 'Grass, rabbit, fox.'

Jade was watching Miss Simpson and listening to her repeating the names of plants and animals and then her voice faded and she heard a different voice in her head. It was still Miss Simpson's but it sounded younger, like the voice of a young girl, a sulky young girl.

'*Why am I doing this? Never wanted to be a teacher. Wanted to be an ice skater. A pro. Could have been, too. Could have been in the Olympics. That's what my coach said. If I hadn't done my hamstring in, doing the splits. Then put on all that weight. Now I have to teach this lot. Look at them. And look at that one. Off with the fairies. Again. Where is she? Not here, that's for sure . . .*'

Too late Jade realized that the voice was talking about her. And a louder voice was breaking through . . . 'Jade?' it was saying, 'Hello-oh? Is anyone there-er?'

Miss Simpson had come right up to her desk and was bending down to peer into her face as if at a small animal in a cage. She knocked on the top of Jade's head. It hurt, quite a lot.

'Ow,' she said.

'Ah. Welcome back to the lesson. Glad you could join us. What was the last thing I just said?'

'Dunno, miss.' She rubbed her head and scowled. The rest of the class watched with interest.

'Dunno, miss. Well of course you don't know. How could you know when you've been staring into space not listening to a single word? You don't know because you weren't listening!'

That was another thing about Miss Simpson. She shouted a lot. Often when she was right in your face. Jade had never liked people who shouted a lot. She wanted to close her eyes and put her hands over her ears.

'Right. Well, this evening you can make up for not listening by writing a thousand words on Woodland Food Chains and if I find you've copied it word for word from the Internet I shall make you write it out all over again. Is that clear?'

'Yes, miss.'

A thousand words! As well as her usual homework. She'd be up all night.

Just because Miss Simpson couldn't be an Olympic ice skater.

She sat there fuming as the teacher walked back to the front of the class.

'Now where was I?' she said.

'*In the middle of an ice rink in a pink tutu and pink boots with pink ribbons in your hair,*' thought Jade angrily. '*Gliding across the ice with hundreds of people watching, hoping you fall through . . .*'

But then she heard snorting and gurgling noises from around the class and Jessica Kingston nudged her in the back and she saw that Miss Simpson was standing staring into space. And one of her feet was kind of sliding across the floor. One leg was slightly bent and she was pushing the other out to the side and then back with this dreamy expression on her face. People were openly smirking and tittering.

Suddenly she seemed to remember where she was.

'Food chains,' she snapped. 'We've only got three. Come on, you can do better than that. Aqueta?'

'Er, nuts, er squirrels, and, and . . . foxes?'

And they were off again.

'Jade?'

'Mushrooms, reindeer and wolves.'

Miss Simpson stared at her as if she was trying to be clever.

'Mushrooms? Reindeer don't eat mushrooms.' She pointed to someone else. 'Kelly?'

'They do, miss, they . . .' But then Jade bit her lip. How did she know reindeer ate mushrooms? She knew nothing about reindeer.

But somehow she just *knew*.

Typical, she thought.

'Leaves, insects and bats,' said Kelly.

Miss Simpson had turned back to the blackboard but now she kind of froze with the chalk in her hand. Slowly she turned round to face the class.

'Anyone else?' she said. 'Omar?'

She doesn't like bats, Jade thought. They scare the pants off her.

She stared at the teacher, but instead of seeing Miss Simpson she saw a little girl with red hair and glasses standing in water up to her knees in a dark, dank cave looking up at a ceiling completely covered with bats.

She felt the picture begin to break up and instinctively she knew that Miss Simpson was fighting it, desperately trying to think of something else. But Jade concentrated. She held the picture together. And she made things happen to it.

She made the bats wake up.

A few of them opened their wings . . . And then the whole ceiling moved and the air was full of thousands of flying, squeaking things . . . Furry, mouse-like bodies, scaly wings, piggy snouts with sharp teeth and narrow piggy eyes . . . diving, darting, squealing . . .

A shriek.

Miss Simpson was ducking and diving and waving her hands around her head.

And then running for the door. Tugging at the handle, pulling it open and hurling herself out into the corridor.

Silence. Stunned silence. Everyone looked at each other in astonishment. Some were grinning as if it was all a big joke but most were too shocked to find it very funny.

Then they all started talking at once.

Except Jade.

She was sitting with her head in her hands

trying to deal with the worst migraine she had ever experienced.

The snake was back and it had brought a few of its friends with it.

6

The Shaman and the Monk

They drove through a blinding snowstorm that hurled itself at the windscreen of the 4 x 4 like a million snow demons trying to get into their heads. Brother Benedict sat hunched over the wheel, peering through the madly racing wipers as the vehicle lurched down the forest track. Beside him sat the shaman Jussa Proksi, a tall, gaunt man of uncertain age – anything between forty and sixty – with a dark beard, streaked with grey, and a weathered complexion that had seen a hundred storms like this and looked like it had been pitted and scoured by most of them.

The shaman could speak English but not comfortably and Benedict was too intent on keeping the vehicle from hitting the trees to have much time for conversation. Finally the snow became too thick and deep even for the 4 x 4 and the shaman suggested they had better take to the snowmobile.

They dragged it off the trailer at the back: a machine that resembled a large motorbike with tracks at the rear and skis at the front. Benedict had never driven one before so he climbed up behind the shaman and they raced on through the forest, almost taking off every time they hit a bump, and skimming the trees by a whisker. After three or four miles they reached the lake.

The waters were well frozen now, with a crust of snow on top of the ice, blown by the wind into the shape of small waves or whipped meringue on an ice-cream cake. But the shaman was loath to take the snowmobile on to the ice and expose them to whoever might be watching from the trees or the castle at the far end of the lake. So they took to the trail skis the shaman had brought with him, following a track that wound around the edge of the lake.

Both men carried rifles and backpacks and it was heavy going in the deep snow. Benedict had used trail skis before but he was no expert – nothing like as skilled as his companion. The trick was to push one ski forward and then slide, push and then slide, but it was tough going on the winding track through the trees. Benedict wore tinted goggles but it was still hard to see the folds and bumps in the ground. Soon he was breathing heavily and sweating in his ski suit despite the cold. After he had taken a couple of tumbles the shaman called a halt and they sat down on a fallen tree. He offered Benedict a sip of Finnish vodka from a hip flask and the monk took the opportunity to ask some of the questions that had been on his mind since he had left Rome.

'Is there no easier way of approaching this place?' he began lightly, handing back the flask and feeling the fiery liquid biting its way down his throat and into his guts.

Jussa Proksi shrugged and for a moment Benedict thought it was the only answer he was going to get. But then he said: 'Is road on Russian side. Is how they bring in stuff for building.'

This was easily the longest sentence he had spoken since they met.

Encouraged, Benedict continued: 'Did you see any of the building work?'

'No.' Then, after a pause . . . 'But I meet with worker in Krasnoborsk – over Russian border.'

He saw Benedict's look of surprise and gave another little shrug. 'I go over border sometime. When I have business in Russia. But is not good place. Is many soldier. Also many gangster and smuggler. Is why we call Badlands.'

The Badlands. So what business did the shaman have there, Benedict wondered?

But all he said was: 'And this worker you met . . .'

'He lose job because he swear at foreman and he is in bar to get drunk. I help him get more drunk.'

Benedict waited patiently while he took another swig of the vodka. The shaman liked a drink himself, he thought. It certainly loosened his tongue.

'He say castle is ruin when they start. They make nine small room – for bedroom maybe – and two, three big one. One is laboratory, he think, in cellar, where is old dungeon. And they fit new door to all cell. Steel door with special lock.'

'Did he know what they were for?'

'No. But they fit iron bar, like cage. He think maybe for animal.'

'What kind of animal?'

'Kind that need bar.' He shook his head. 'He not know.'

'Did he have any idea what it was they were building?'

'He think maybe hotel – for conference.'

'A hotel? With cells? And cages? And a laboratory?'

The shaman shrugged again. 'Maybe they lock up guest when they want leave. Maybe they make experiment with them. Is mystery, yes.'

'So he had no idea who was employing him?'

'He work for contractor. Not owner direct. But I check with land register, back in Finland. Castle is military building. Even old ruin like this. And Ruski and Finn they have deal. Any work on military building near border they tell. So the Ruski tell about Castle Piru. Is study centre, they say, for education. And owner is name СеМИлéТКА – education charity based Moscow.'

'*Semeeletka?*' Benedict repeated thoughtfully.

'Is mean Seven Year Plan – or School. You know?'

'No. No, I'm sorry, please go on.'

'Is no more tell. You ready go now?'

They pressed on. From time to time Benedict caught sight of the lake through the trees. Then the shaman pulled up sharply in front of him and, startled, he glimpsed the head and horns of a large animal through the falling snow.

He reached for the gun on his shoulder. But it was only the head and horns. The grisly remains of what had once been a reindeer.

They were impaled on the point of a long spear. One end buried in the snow; the other – the sharp end – protruding from the head just between the antlers, like an extra horn.

Jussa Proksi approached it cautiously and walked around it twice in a small circle then he nodded as if it provided the answer to something that had been puzzling him.

'Is Salmmo,' he said. 'Tapio bull.'

This meant nothing to Benedict.

'Tapio is one who go missing,' said the shaman.

'How you can tell this was his bull?' Benedict was incredulous.

'I know him many year this bull,' said the shaman. 'Besides, I know mark on ear.'

He showed Benedict how the right ear had been clipped in a particular way.

'Every farm has mark. So at round-up we know what is own reindeer and what belong some other. But Salmmo, I know like old friend. And this is all they leave of him,' he added sadly.

Benedict looked about him on each side of the

track but there was no sign of the slaughter. Anything that remained had been hidden by the falling snow.

'You say "they"?'

'Whoever kill him. Is not animal. Not animal we know.'

'And why would they leave the head?'

'As warning. Against trespass.'

Benedict shook his head in bewilderment. 'Wouldn't a notice have done? Trespassers will be prosecuted. In several different languages.'

'Whoever do this, they know *Sami. Sami* is not afraid of many thing but this evil thing. They keep away.'

'You think this is something to do with the castle – and whoever is there now?'

'I not know. But this . . . we not see before. When castle is ruin.'

He began to mutter what Benedict took to be some kind of incantation and he made a sign in the air that was not quite the sign of the cross. Then astonishingly he took the hip flask out of his pocket, unscrewed the cap, took a brief swig and then poured a little over the head of the dead bull.

'What are you doing?' asked Benedict.

The shaman did not answer but only said: 'We go

on. And Old Salmmo guard our back.'

But they had scarcely taken a few steps when they saw something else through the trees — a crude structure of rope and logs.

'What is it?' Benedict asked. He thought it might be another fetish — a warning sign — like the head of the reindeer.

'Bear trap,' said the shaman. He shook his head. 'Bad. Is forbid.'

He went up close while Benedict stared about him through the trees.

'Something is catch,' said the shaman. 'Not long. Something big.'

He pointed to the scratch marks on the logs, deep gouges in the wood. Then he stooped and picked up something else that he had seen part buried in the snow. It looked like a kind of charm on a silver chain.

'Aslat,' he said softly.

'Aslat?'

'Aslat Turi. Tapio son. They go find Salmmo and his herd. I think they find them — and something else.'

'Are you sure? I mean, that this is . . .'

'I give him when he is ten,' he said. 'For birthday.'

They went on in silence, trudging through the deep snow. The ground had begun to rise slightly.

'We reach fell at end of lake,' Jussa Proksi said. 'Is steep climb from here. But we look down on castle, I think.'

They struggled on for another half-hour with the ground becoming steadily steeper. Then finally they saw the lake again through the trees, several hundred metres below.

And there was the castle rising like a great black rock through the falling snow.

They moved to the edge of the cliff, but stayed under cover of the trees. The castle was about three or four hundred metres below them, on a small island with a bridge linking it to the shore. It comprised a single square tower five or six floors high with a turret at each corner and several smaller buildings clustered at the foot of the walls. The only sign of life was a thin smudge of smoke rising from one of the chimneys.

Benedict snapped his boots out of the skis and squatted down, taking the pack off his shoulders and groping inside to find his camera. He had to take off his goggles and his gloves, and his fingers froze on the cold metal. He took several wide shots and then zoomed in for some close-ups of the battlements and turrets. Then he felt an urgent hand on his shoulder.

'See,' murmured the shaman. 'On roof.'

Benedict looked and saw a dark shape on the battlements. It was standing quite still and appeared to be hunched up with its head bowed, as if it was praying. He aimed his camera again and zoomed in as far as he could but then, instead of taking the shot, he peered through the viewfinder in astonishment. For it was no human figure that he could see at the end of the zoom. It was a bear.

Even in the low light with the falling snow Benedict could not mistake it. And as he watched, it moved off with its shambling gait around the corner of the turret and he just had time to knock off a couple of shots before it disappeared from sight.

He took his eyes from the viewfinder and turned to Jussa Proksi – but before he could speak the shaman pointed again and, following the line of his outstretched finger, Benedict saw another figure on the far side of the battlements. He looked through the viewfinder again, at maximum zoom, but this figure was different. Even at the greater distance Benedict could see that it wore a long robe with a hood or cowl, like an old-fashioned monk, and it was looking away from them, out over the lake. Then, as Benedict began to click the shutter, the figure turned in his direction. The cowl and the falling snow and the low light made it impossible to see a face, and Benedict felt that he was staring into a dark hole – but he had the alarming thought that whatever it was under the grim cowl, it was staring straight back at him. *And that it was someone he knew.*

Benedict froze. But it was surely impossible for the figure to see him so far away through the snow and the trees.

Then he heard something. It was distant but it sounded to Benedict very much like the bellowing of a bull.

'Salmmo,' said the shaman.

Benedict stared at him.

'Salmmo?' he repeated. 'But Salmmo is dead.'

Very dead. Just a head impaled on a spear.

'I ask him guard our back. And now he warn us. Come. Quick.'

Benedict struggled back into his skis and followed the shaman through the trees, fighting a growing sense of unreality.

They skied down the slope of the fell, clumsily steering a path through the trees, and they had almost reached level ground when they heard another sound – so eerie and menacing that despite the hood

Benedict wore over his head he felt the hairs rise on the back of his neck.

The howling of wolves.

They carried on through the trees at the edge of the lake but Benedict was still finding it difficult to move at any pace on the level ground and the howls were getting closer.

Jussa Proksi stopped and shouted back at him.

'We go on lake.'

Benedict raised a hand in acknowledgement and followed him through the trees, struggling to stay upright on his skis.

They emerged about half a mile from the castle but it was almost hidden by the falling snow and the light was fading fast. They moved on to the ice and Benedict found it a little easier. But they still had a long way to go, and as he looked back over his shoulder he saw them. The lean, dark shapes breaking cover and starting out after them across the lake.

He slipped the rifle from his shoulders.

'You go on,' he shouted. 'I'll hold them off.'

But the shaman was already lying down and taking careful aim.

The wolves came steadily on. Great timber wolves, bigger than any Benedict had seen in Europe. Eight or nine of them, closing in with deadly purpose. He could see the grey-white ruffs on their powerful necks, the lolling tongues and the black slits of their eyes. Then the shaman fired and the leader turned a backward somersault over the ice.

But then incredibly it was up and still coming on.

The shaman raised his eyes from the sights of his rifle. He looked at the weapon in astonishment and then at Benedict.

No time for a discussion about it. Benedict lined it up in his sights at about a hundred metres and squeezed the trigger. The animal went down and this time it stayed down. He fired three more rounds in rapid succession and hit two more of the brutes. One shot left and no time to reload. But the wolves were no longer running towards them. The six survivors had sheered off to one side and stopped, crouched on their bellies, tongues lolling, lying low in the ice.

'Come,' said the shaman.

Benedict followed him across the lake, thrusting powerfully with the poles and almost skating now across the ice. He glanced back several times and saw that the wolves were following them – but at a safe distance. They reached the snowmobile and the shaman loaded their skis on the back while Benedict kept guard. It was difficult to see the wolves now in the poor light – they were like shadows flitting across the folds of snow – but he fancied they were creeping closer.

The shaman revved the engine and Benedict leaped on the back, still clutching his rifle. But it was impossible to drive at speed with so many roots and broken branches lying hidden under the snow, and looking back over his shoulder Benedict saw the wolves had resumed the chase.

And then suddenly a snarling fury burst through the trees on his left and hurled itself at him.

He had a brief image of fur and flying snow, black wolf eyes and yellow fangs flecked with foam. And then he brought the rifle up with both hands and caught the beast under the jaw and sent it tumbling back with a yelp into the trees.

Jussa Proksi opened the throttle in reckless disregard for roots, branches or whatever else might lie in their path and they hurtled through the forest at breakneck speed. At times they appeared to be flying. They would hit a particularly steep incline and take off, landing with a jolt that shook every bone in Benedict's body and threatened to hurl him into the path of the pursuing wolves. Low branches swept their heads; others flew up from beneath the front skis. But the gods of the forest were on their side – doubtless recruited like the long-dead reindeer by the shaman's prayers – and they swiftly pulled ahead. And in a while, peering over the shaman's shoulder, Benedict saw the welcome shape of the 4 x 4 in the beam of the single headlight through the trees.

They almost hurled the heavy snowmobile on to the trailer and Benedict took the wheel of the Audi, gunning it down the forest track at a pace he would never have dared attempt earlier.

Jussa Proksi reached into his pocket for the half-empty flask of vodka.

'I never see wolf like that,' he said, when he had taken a long draught and coughed some air back into his lungs. 'I never hear they attack people before, not in Finland. Not so big. And I hit one, you see? And still he come. What kind of wolves do this?'

'Werewolves?' proposed Benedict with a smile.

The shaman regarded him with suspicion as he hunched over the wheel, concentrating on steering them through the rushing avenue of trees. 'But you hit and they stay down. What kind gun you use – what kind bullet?'

'Nothing special,' said Benedict, who had his own secret spells and did not plan to reveal them to Jussa Proksi or any mortal man. 'I must have got lucky. Or maybe it was the Hail Marys.'

But the silver bullets he had used were very special and he, too, wondered at the nature of these animals. And what dark arts had preserved them from normal bullets.

And he wondered about the shrouded figure he had seen on the battlements of the castle and what it would do when its creatures came trooping back, their mission unaccomplished, across the frozen waters of the lake.

7

The Godmother

'Miss Simpson isn't feeling too good,' said Mr Coleridge, 'so I'll be taking you for the rest of the day.'

Grins all round. Mr Coleridge was the deputy head but he was a pussycat after Miss Simpson.

He noticed Jade was sitting with her head in her hands.

'She's got a headache, sir,' said Miriam Forsythe, who'd been fussing over her, making it worse.

'Jade, is that right?'

'Yes, sir,' whispered Jade. She didn't feel like explaining that it was a migraine. She didn't think she could even *say* migraine.

'I see. Well, you'd better go and lie down in the first-aid room for a while.'

* * *

Jade lay on the bed in the first-aid room feeling sorry for herself. She even felt sorry for Miss Simpson. But whatever it was she'd done to her she was paying the price for it now. Miss Simpson's head might be full of bats but her own was full of snakes, all with the same zigzag pattern on their backs, wriggling across her left eye. And even when she kept both eyes shut they were still there, as if she was looking down into a deep dark pit and they were writhing and coiling in the bottom of it.

And in the darkness behind the snakes there was something else. What was it? A shadow, a darker patch within the darkness. She couldn't really see it; it was more as if she could sense it. And with it a feeling of coldness; of a cold, desolate place with something weird and threatening and . . .

She felt a presence in the room and opened her eyes in alarm – but it was only Miss Wylie, the school secretary, who was in charge of first aid.

'How are you feeling?' she asked, laying her hand on Jade's forehead.

'I think it's a migraine,' whispered Jade. She was surprised she could get the words out.

'Do you often get migraines?' Miss Wylie asked.

She looked concerned.

She shook her head – slowly and carefully, so it wouldn't fall off.

Only when I read people's minds, she thought. Only when I attack teachers with bats.

How had she done it? It was as if she could see a picture of what was in Miss Simpson's mind: in her deepest, innermost thoughts. But more than that . . . she could *change* the picture. Add a few touches of her own here and there and send it back.

But never again, she thought. I promise I will never, ever do that again.

It was a promise she sincerely meant to keep.

'I think I'd better phone your parents,' said Miss Wylie, 'and get one of them to pick you up.'

Jade nodded. She dreaded the thought of doing lessons – or even having anyone talk to her. As the snakes faded the headache came on. All she wanted to do was lie down with her eyes closed in darkness and complete silence and not move.

After a few minutes Miss Wylie came back.

'Your mother's coming for you,' she said softly. 'She'll be here in a few minutes.'

But it wasn't Jade's mother. It was her Aunt Em.

'Hello, you,' she said, not unkindly. 'So what's

all this about?'

Jade squinted at her in surprise.

'What are *you* doing here?' she said feebly.

Aunt Em wasn't really Jade's aunt — she was her godmother. Her mother's oldest friend. Sometimes Jade thought she was her mother's *only* friend and even then they didn't seem to see much of each other. They'd been best friends at school, her mother said, though Jade couldn't think how; they were like chalk and cheese.

'I called round for a coffee,' she said, 'and the school rang so I told your mother I'd go fetch you.'

She spoke with a faint American accent. She'd been born in New York and only came over to England in her teens. Now she lived on the other side of London, in Docklands, and her visits were usually arranged well in advance.

If Aunt Em was round at Jade's house it was for a reason. And Jade had a dim idea in the murky depths of her troubled brain that the reason was her.

She sat down on the chair next to the first-aid bed and put her hand on Jade's forehead. Unlike Miss Wylie's hand it was cool and soothing and Jade was sorry when she took it away.

'You do seem to have a bit of a temperature,' she said.

Aunt Em's real name was *Doctor* Emily Mortlake but she wasn't a family doctor or a surgeon; she was a scientist and her particular field was genetics. Aunt Em had explained genetics to her once when she'd just turned nine but she might have missed some of the finer points. It came from the ancient Greek word for giving birth and it was the science of genes or heredity – the characteristics you inherited from your parents, including their diseases. She said she was working on something called the genetic code, which was of vital importance to the future of medicine – and humankind for that matter – but Jade found it confusing at the best of times and couldn't even bear to think about it now.

'Well, if you think you can walk,' she said, 'I think we'd better get you home.'

She helped Jade totter across to the car park. She had a new car since Jade last saw her – a red coupé.

'Cool car,' said Jade faintly. She wasn't in the best mood to appreciate it. She appreciated the soft leather seats, though, when she sank into them.

'It's an Alfa,' said Aunt Em as she turned the ignition.

Jade opened one eye and squinted up at her. Aunt Em knew a lot about cars. In fact she seemed to know a lot about most things. She was the same age as Jade's mother, which was thirty-eight, but she looked at least five years younger. (This, according to Jade's mother, was because she had a lot more money and no kids.) Like Jade she had short blonde hair but it didn't stick up every which way like Jade's did and though she hardly wore any make-up she always looked perfectly groomed. Today she was wearing a suit in a mossy-green material and a pair of suede boots the same colour, and round her neck she wore a thin gold necklace with a stone pendant that might be jade. Jade had a necklace like it at home that Aunt Em had given her soon after she was born but she was only allowed to wear it on special occasions.

They swung through the school gates and Jade groaned and closed her eyes again and didn't open them until they arrived home.

'Good heavens, you're white as a sheet,' her mother said when she saw her. She looked worried and a bit scared. 'Is it a migraine?'

Jade saw the look she gave Aunt Em, as if for reassurance, or confirmation.

'I think she's over the worst,' said Aunt Em.

'Why don't you go and lie down in your bedroom,' said her mother, 'and I'll come up in a few minutes.'

But in fact it was Aunt Em who came up — with a glass of water and a paracetamol.

'Take this,' she said. 'Your mom phoned the doctor and he said it would be all right for now. But if you get another migraine she'll have to take you to see him.'

She sat down on the side of the bed and watched Jade as she took her pill.

'She says you keep getting these things. Any idea what brings them on?'

'Dunno,' said Jade.

'Problems at school?'

They always asked that if you were depressed or feeling ill but it never stopped them sending you there.

Jade shook her head. She could do it now without worrying about her head falling off. She began to perk up a bit.

'Not being bullied or anything?'

'No.'

'None of the teachers picking on you?'

'Not really.'

She didn't want to go into the problem of Miss

Simpson right now. Besides, she'd dealt with that in her own way.

'And there's nothing on your mind? Nothing you want to ask about?'

What did she mean, *nothing you want to ask about?*

There were tons of things she wanted to ask about. Perhaps this was her big chance. Aunt Em would get a lot more than she bargained for. But no. Maybe not. You often got more than you bargained for from Aunt Em; a bit too much detail. It might bring back the migraine.

She shook her head and Aunt Em nodded as if she was satisfied but she kept looking at Jade in that thoughtful way she had. She didn't really know how to deal with Jade and sometimes they were a bit uneasy with each other. Her mother said she was very fond of her but didn't know how to show it. She didn't have any children of her own. Jade had an idea she'd been married once when she was quite young but it hadn't lasted very long. They'd never talked about it.

'Your mom says the head teacher thinks you're very bright.'

Jade said nothing. It wasn't what Miss Simpson said. What Miss Simpson said was *You're too clever for your own good, my girl.*

'But she also says you get bored very easily. Is that true?'

Jade shrugged. 'Sometimes.'

'In fact, she reckons you'd be better off at a special school. A school that can give you a bit more than they can.'

Jade was instantly suspicious. 'What sort of special school?' she demanded.

'A school for gifted children.'

Now Jade knew why Aunt Em had called round for coffee.

'What does "gifted" mean?' Jade knew very well what it meant but she wanted to hear what Aunt Em had to say about it.

'Children who are particularly bright and intelligent. Children who tend to get bored with school work because it's too easy for them. Children who need a bit more of a challenge.'

Jade didn't like the sound of that. It sounded like another way of saying, Children who need to work harder.

Still, it was true that she was bored – and not only with school work.

'Would it mean going away?'

'Well, it *might* mean that. Would you *mind* going

away – I mean, to boarding school?'

Jade considered. She didn't know anyone at boarding school but if you could believe the books you read the kids who went there had a pretty good time. She and her friends had discussed it and were almost equally divided. Half of them thought it would be cool to live away from home with kids their own age. The other half thought they would miss their parents and their brothers and sisters. Not having any brothers or sisters Jade was inclined to favour the cool argument.

'Well, no need to make a decision in a hurry,' said Aunt Em, 'but perhaps we'll think about it, shall we?'

Jade nodded and Aunt Em sighed and stood up.

'And don't worry about anything,' she said, now that she'd given Jade something else to worry about. 'We don't want to bring any more migraines on, do we?'

But Jade knew that her migraine had nothing to do with worrying. They were to do with the voices she heard and the pictures she saw – from inside people's heads.

She eased herself off the bed and crossed to the window, walking on egg shells in case she started the migraine off again. It was just turning dark. A crushing feeling of boredom came over her at the thought of the long evening that stretched ahead.

She saw Aunt Em emerge from the front door and walk towards her car. She looked up at the window and though Jade didn't have the light on she must have seen her standing there because she raised her hand and fluttered her fingers in an awkward wave. Jade raised her hand in acknowledgement. She had a sudden almost overwhelming urge to go with her. To her flat in Docklands or wherever else she was going for the evening. But she was probably going back to work. She was a workaholic, her mother said.

She watched her get into the car and pull out into the road. And then, just as Jade was about to turn away, she saw another car pull out from the line of parked cars on the opposite side and head off in the same direction.

She didn't seriously think Aunt Em was being followed, though the thought did flash through her mind — she'd seen movies or police series where this kind of thing happened — but not in Turnham Green . . .

But as the car drove away she saw a face in the rear window.

It was the face of a man. Not a man she

recognized; not, at least, from this distance and at this angle. But whoever he was, he was twisted round in the back seat of the car and he was peering straight up at her.

8

The Castle of the Angel

Brother Benedict gazed down through the narrow window of the Castel Sant' Angelo high above the River Tiber in Rome.

A dank, wintry mist hung low over the city, hiding the modern office blocks and muting the sound of traffic. All he could see were the statues of the angels on the bridge, rising above the mist as if ascending through clouds, and one of the Swiss guards in the courtyard below, dressed in the traditional blue-and-yellow uniform of the corps and armed with an ancient pike.

They could have been back in the Middle Ages.

'A school, you say?' mused the Knight Commander as he studied the pictures on the screen of his computer.

'That's what the shaman said,' Benedict corrected him mildly. He turned from the window and crossed to the desk so he could look over the Commander's shoulder at the pictures of the castle in the snow.

'It would have to be a very special kind of school,' he added, 'to be located in a castle on a frozen lake in the middle of nowhere.'

'But then it would be for a very special kind of pupil,' the Commander replied mysteriously. He scrolled to the next shot, a blurred image of the cowled figure on the battlements.

'And they call it the Place of Demons?'

'Apparently so. Guarding the gates of Hell.'

'An apt choice then.'

Benedict shrugged slightly. 'If it's our man,' he said.

'Oh, I don't think there can be any doubt about that,' said the Commander complacently. 'No doubt at all.'

He moved to the next shot. A wider angle, showing the castle in its setting on the frozen lake with the forest all around and the fir trees powdered with snow.

'A castle and a bridge,' he mused. 'Almost a mirror image of our own situation here in Rome. By intention, do you think?'

'It would appeal to his conceit,' said the monk.

He moved back to the window and looked down at the guard as he stamped his feet on the frozen cobbles of the courtyard. The Castel Sant' Angelo had been built by the ancient Romans as a tomb for the Emperor Hadrian but it had served as a fortress for over fifteen hundred years – and a refuge for the Popes in times of seige. Whoever held the castle, it was said, held Rome.

It was a museum now but it still had the appearance of a fortress and the Commander clearly felt at home here. The building was a labyrinth of rooms and corridors, many of them unused for years and unknown to the casual visitor.

A perfect place for two men who had secrets to discuss.

The Commander was not dressed as a military man. He wore a dark, beautifully cut suit with a white shirt and tie, and the only sign of his calling was a small lapel badge bearing the insignia of the Order: a white cross on a black background crowned by the scallop shell of the faithful who had made the pilgrimage to Jerusalem in the Middle Ages. Benedict was dressed far more casually in T-shirt and jeans and a black leather jacket with a hood. The T-shirt was also black and there was a small white cross on the pocket directly above his heart.

The office, at least, was more traditional. A suit of armour stood in one corner and various weapons – swords, shields and battleaxes – were displayed on the walls. Behind the Commander's desk was the battle standard of the Order, much tattered and stained, and above the ancient stone fireplace hung a large painting of the Knights at the Battle of Buda in 1510 when they had charged across the frozen waters of Lake Negus in the war against the Turks.

Father Johann would have recognized those Knights. They were dressed exactly like the vision he had seen at the door of his presbytery when Brother Benedict stepped out from his car into the snow.

'I want you to read something,' the Commander said. 'Something that is known only to myself, the Grand Master, and a small number of people outside the Order.'

He selected a file from his Personal folder and entered a code on the keyboard.

'Those who do know of it call it the Rackthorne Experiment.'

He invited the monk to sit at his desk and took his place by the window.

The mist was thinning. He could see patches of pale-blue sky and a wintry sun . . . and on the bridge below a group of tourists making their way towards the castle gates, led by a guide carrying an umbrella.

Thousands of tourists visited the castle every year and heard why it was called the Castle of the Angel.

The story went back to the sixth century when a terrible plague had swept through the city, slaying people in their thousands. Pope Gregory had led a procession through the streets, chanting prayers for deliverance, and as they were crossing the bridge he looked up and saw an angel on the stone ramparts of the castle sheathing his sword. And he took it as a sign that their ordeal was at an end.

The castle and its bronze angel had guarded Rome ever since. Even when Rome was sacked by foreign armies the castle had never fallen.

One of the tour party aimed his camera and the Commander instinctively stepped back into the shadows. It was just another tourist site to them, a piece of ancient history, its battles long over. But not to the Commander. For him the battles would never be over.

He saw that Benedict had finished reading.

'Monstrous, don't you think?' he said.

The monk nodded, though he did not look particularly horrified – or even surprised – at what he had read.

'What became of the children?' he asked.

'We don't know,' the Commander admitted. 'Not in the majority of cases. However . . .' he hesitated and gazed for a moment at the picture above the fireplace as if seeking inspiration from the charging knights. It would have been far easier in the old days, he reflected, when the Order had greater earthly powers and ruled over vast territories. In those days the Grand Master and the Knight Commanders made decisions that could mean life or death for millions.

'We believe these "experiments" to be the work of the Devil,' he continued, 'and that . . . that they must be prevented from reaching any kind of . . . fruition.'

Benedict was watching him carefully. He had eyes that seemed to change as they caught the light, something between grey and blue – like the mist, the Commander thought, as it rose from the river. And like a mist they seemed to mask his thoughts.

'We want you to go to London,' said the Knight

Commander, 'to find a child – a girl child. And, let us say, remove her from temptation. It is not something I ask lightly of you, but will you do it?'

'I am a servant of the Order,' said Brother Benedict with a small bow. 'And I will carry out its commands to the best of my ability – whatever they may be.'

9

Kidnapped

It was Saturday morning and Jade was on the computer in her bedroom. She was supposed to be doing her homework – the extra homework she had been given by Miss Simpson – but instead she was trying to find out about the place where she had been born.

'Rackthorne,' she read, 'began as a place where three tracks met in the Royal Forest of Windsor. But in the last fifty years the village has grown enormously as a result of its proximity to London and Heathrow Airport. Many new housing estates have been built and Rackthorne has become a desirable place to live . . .'

Blah de blah. She scrolled down to the bottom of

the page and was about to click on Images when she came to something more interesting, at least from her point of view:

'The village is the site of Houndwood Hospital, originally named Houndwood Criminal Lunatic Asylum, for patients of "dangerous, violent or criminal nature". As a result of local concerns, seven sirens were set up in the village which sound for twenty minutes when there is an escape. The village is ringed with roadblocks and the police check every vehicle for the missing patient. The sirens are tested every Monday morning.'

Jade wondered if it would have been more exciting to have stayed in Rackthorne instead of moving to Turnham Green but decided, on balance, it would not. This was not the kind of excitement she was looking for. It sounded just like Turnham Green except that sirens went off every Monday morning.

She was about to click on to 'English Woodland Animals' to see what it had to say about food chains when a small box appeared in the bottom right-hand corner of the screen. This was unusual – Jade's computer was programmed to block pop-ups – and she was about to click on Exit when she saw the picture.

It was the castle on the frozen lake.

It had disappeared as a screen display but now it was back as a pop-up – and with a question.

Where am I? Guess right and win a thousand pounds!

Normally she would have treated such an offer with the contempt it deserved but for once she was tempted. If only to find out who was sending it to her. She clicked the mouse and the full-screen image appeared again with a box that invited her to type in her answer.

The castle suggested somewhere in Europe, and the snow and the ice meant it had to be in the north. Scotland, possibly, or Denmark. But then she remembered the sound she'd heard – the howling of a wolf. No wolves in either of those countries. Further north then. Norway, Sweden, Finland . . . or Russia. She knew there were wolves in Russia.

She was about to type it into the box when the voice in her head said: '*Finland, dummy.*'

Jade shrugged. Who cares? Finland, she typed.

You are right!!!! Enter name and address to win £1,000!!!!!

Yeah, sure, she thought. She wasn't that stupid.

She looked for the Exit but there wasn't one. This was annoying. She had to press Alt and Del to get rid of it.

Then she heard someone coming up the stairs and hastily clicked on to English Woodland Animals. Seconds later she heard her mother's voice.

'Doing your homework?'

'Yes,' said Jade without turning round. She scrolled down to bats. She was going to put in every English bat she could find – with pictures.

'I hope you're not just copying it straight from the computer.'

Jade rolled her eyes.

'Well, when you've got a minute can I have a word?'

Jade swung round on her chair.

This was not like her mother. Normally it was: 'Jade! I want a word with you. Stop that and watch my lips.'

She suspected a degree of sarcasm but no, she seemed perfectly sincere, if a little nervous.

'I've just had a call from your Aunt Em,' she said. 'She wants to take you out.'

Jade frowned. This wasn't exactly routine either. 'Out where?' she demanded.

'I don't know exactly.'

This meant she did but wouldn't say.

'She'll tell you when she gets here.'

'She's coming here *now*?'

'She'll be here in five minutes. I didn't think you'd mind. As it's Saturday morning and you're not doing anything in particular.'

Tell me about it.

'And you can do your homework tomorrow, at the last possible moment. Like you usually do.'

This was more like her mother.

'OK.' Jade shrugged and looked out the window to see what the weather was doing. Low grey clouds, hint of rain. Typical November weather. She was wearing scruffy old jeans and a sweater. Aunt Em might be taking her somewhere posh but hey, they should have told her. She put on her boots and her leather jacket and as an afterthought the baker's boy cap her Aunt Em had bought her on her last birthday. She was trying different angles in the mirror when the doorbell rang and she clumped down the stairs.

She was vaguely surprised that she wasn't sent back up again to change but though Aunt Em eyed her a bit critically, for once she didn't say anything and even her mother was strangely quiet on the subject of Jade's appearance.

'Where we going?' Jade asked when they were in the car.

'Wait and see,' said Aunt Em predictably. She stuck a CD on. Opera. Great, thought Jade. A Magical Mystery Tour with Torture.

But then, after a few minutes, Aunt Em said: 'I'm taking you to see a school.'

Even better. Just what she'd wanted to do on a Saturday morning.

'What kind of school?'

'The kind we were talking about the other day. Do you mind?'

It was a bit late for that, Jade thought, when they were already on their way. She also thought it was a bit strange that Aunt Em was taking her there and not her parents. But she didn't say either of these things. She just asked how far it was.

'Oh, not far,' said Aunt Em vaguely. 'And we're only going to look at it. We're not going to meet anybody or anything.'

Which was presumably why she didn't care what Jade was wearing.

Jade stared out of the window. They were turning down the slip road toward the M4, heading west out of the city.

'Is it in the country?' she asked . . .

And then a number of things happened very

quickly. So quickly it was only afterwards that she started to piece them together. At the time they were more of a blur, a long drawn-out scream of squealing tyres and smashing glass and shouting and swear words and sprays of paint and blood . . .

She had been vaguely conscious of the van that overtook them on the slip road. Perhaps Aunt Em swore – or perhaps that was a moment later when it swerved in front of them and slammed on its brakes. Jade lurched forward and was brought up with a jerk by her seat belt. They skidded off the road on to the hard shoulder.

'What . . . ?' she began . . . But then she just stared with her mouth open.

A number of men were piling out of the back of the van.

If they *were* men.

They were wearing masks. Animal masks. A fox, a badger, a hedgehog . . .

Animals of the English Woodland. The nightmare.

Then they were all around them with paint cans, spraying bright-red paint all over the windscreen and Aunt Em was twisting round in her seat and reversing and then . . . Bang! She hit something. Another van had pulled up behind them. And then the window on

Jade's side exploded inwards with a shower of glass and a face appeared in the gap . . . the face of a squirrel.

Jade yelled and lashed out at it. But it just leaned in and opened the door and hit the release on her seat belt. She turned to hold on to Aunt Em but Aunt Em was half in and half out of the car struggling with someone in a fox mask.

Still yelling, Jade was dragged out into the road. Squirrel-face clamped a hand over her mouth and she bit it — so hard she tasted blood. He drew back his fist to smash into her face and then suddenly the motorbike was there.

It came roaring up on the hard shoulder and crashed right into the squirrel, sending him reeling against the car and a voice shouted 'Jump on!'

Jade looked to see what Aunt Em was doing.

She was kicking fox-face in the balls.

'Go, go, go!' she yelled at Jade.

So Jade jumped up on the back of the bike and they went — scattering Animals of the English Woodland in all directions, swerving round the white van . . . and hurtling down the M4 like a bat out of Miss Simpson's own private Hell.

10

The Place in the Forest

Jade had never ridden on a motorbike before. At first she held on to the rider's belt and sat well back in the saddle, trying to keep as far apart from him as possible, but he was hunched over the fuel tank and the ice-cold wind spilled over the tiny windscreen and over his shoulders and hit her full in the face, bringing tears to her eyes. She was forced to lean forward with her arms wrapped round his waist and her face pressed into his leather jacket.

She was just beginning to get the hang of it when they turned off the motorway and pulled up at the side of the road.

The biker helped Jade off the back and took off his

helmet. He was young with long blond hair and designer stubble. Quite fit.

'Sorry about that,' he said, 'but I couldn't think of anything else to do.'

'That's all right,' said Jade graciously. Then she remembered to say thank you. After all he *had* saved her life – or something like that. She was shaking. She must be in shock.

'Who were they?' she said. 'What did they want?'

And who was *he*?

She couldn't think straight. It didn't help that they seemed to be on the main flight path for Heathrow Airport. She ducked as a jumbo jet screamed low over their heads.

'We should call the police,' she said, when she could hear herself speak. Then her phone rang and she fumbled to reach it inside her leather jacket.

It was Aunt Em, sounding a little less cool than she usually did. But at least she was alive.

'Jade, is that you? Are you all right – where are you?'

'I'm OK. I'm in a lay-by off the M4.' Jade tried to sound perfectly calm and matter-of-fact. 'What happened – are *you* OK?'

'Don't worry about me, I'm fine but . . .' The rest

was lost in the sound of another flight coming in. Great place to stop, Jade thought. When she could hear again Aunt Em was still asking where she was.

'I'm with the man on the motorbike,' said Jade.

'I know. Let me speak to him.'

Mystified, Jade held out the phone.

'My Aunt Emily wants to speak to you,' she said.

The man took the phone and to Jade's annoyance walked away with it so she couldn't hear what he was saying. Not that he was saying much – just listening. After a couple of minutes he came back and handed her the phone. Aunt Em was still there.

'Jade – I want you to listen to me very carefully,' she said. 'Barney is going to take you somewhere safe.'

'Barney?'

'The man you're with.'

Jade turned her back on him, just as he had on her.

'Who is he?' she hissed.

'He's one of my young men. You can trust him.'

One of her young men? How many did she have?

'Where's he taking me?'

'Somewhere safe,' Aunt Em repeated unhelpfully. 'I'll be there as soon as I can.'

'But who were they – what did they want?' Jade

repeated. Why wouldn't people tell her what was going on?

'I don't know — yet. We'll talk about it when I see you.'

'But hadn't I better call my mum?'

'I've already called her. She's going to ring you. But, Jade, it's very important you do exactly what we say at the moment till we find out what's going on, do you understand me?'

'Yes but . . .'

'Trust me, Jade, just trust me. I'll be with you shortly.'

Another plane came over and when it had gone so had Aunt Em.

Jade didn't know what to think. She wondered if she should phone her mother right away but while she was standing there still trying to make up her mind the phone rang again and it was her.

'Oh Jade, what have you got us into now?' she began, and her voice lapsed into a familiar whine . . . 'This is all too much for me. I don't think I can cope any more.'

Excuse me? It wasn't her mother who'd been attacked by a crowd of walk-ons from Disneyland.

'There were all these men,' Jade told her,

'with animal masks . . .'

'I know, I know,' she said wearily. 'Emily has told me all about it.'

Well, that's all right then.

'I lost my hat,' said Jade and suddenly she found herself shaking and having to fight back the tears. 'Shouldn't we phone the police?'

'I'm sure Emily's taken care of that. Now, Jade, you must do exactly what she tells you, do you understand?'

Honestly, you'd have thought Aunt Em was the head of the family or something. But her mother sometimes seemed to think she was. Em thinks this, Em thinks that . . . Her father called her the Duchess but even he went along with it.

Jade dropped her voice. 'I'm with this guy on a motorbike,' she said.

Her mother hated motorbikes. She'd have had a fit if Jade had gone anywhere near one – before today.

'I know. Aunt Em said. Hold on tight.'

Hold on tight. Is that all she had to say?

'But where's he taking me?'

She repeated the Aunt Em mantra . . . 'Somewhere safe. We'll be there as fast as we can. Your father's coming home from the office.'

And that was it.

Barney the Biker opened a box on the back and took out a crash helmet.

'Try this for size,' he said.

It was almost an exact fit. She wondered if he'd chosen it specially for her. Or perhaps Aunt Em had. Obviously he'd been following Aunt Em's car – in case something like this happened?

Aunt Em thought of everything.

They kept to the back roads, skirting Heathrow, and there seemed to be a roundabout every few hundred metres. It was like a particularly unpleasant ride at the funfair . . . and she kept remembering details of what had happened, like flashbacks. The men in masks piling out of the van, the paint sprays, the window exploding inwards and the man in the squirrel mask grabbing her . . .

She could hardly complain about life being boring – not at the moment anyway – but she wished she knew what was happening and where they were heading.

They came up to another roundabout and as she leaned into the turn she glimpsed a name on the road sign. A name she recognized.

Rackthorne.

She felt her stomach lurch, even more than when they went into the corners. As if it had been waiting for her all along, like some place in a horror movie.

They were clear of the airport now and travelling through quiet countryside. Hedgerows flashed past on both sides of the road and she caught a glimpse of fields, drab and empty at this time of the year, and once a herd of cows chewing at things that looked like human heads in the mud. Probably turnips but the way things were going she wouldn't have been surprised if they *were* heads. Then they were speeding down a long straight stretch of road through what looked like a thick forest.

'. . . *a place where three tracks met in the Royal Forest of Windsor . . .*'

It went on for miles and finally she shut her eyes because the sense of the trees rushing past made her feel giddy. When she opened them Barney was slowing down and they were cruising past large houses set back from the road among pines and Jade saw a sign that read: Welcome to Rackthorne.

Jade felt curious and frightened at the same time. But why should she be frightened by the place where she had been born?

And then they slowed right down and turned left

into a long drive and at the end of it there was a building that looked like a castle gatehouse with battlements and a great wooden door . . . and a large sign next to it that said Houndwood Hospital.

The hospital for the criminally insane.

11

The Annex

High brick walls topped by razor wire. Heavy metal gates that slid open and shut behind her. CCTV cameras and floodlights and uniformed guards.

Through the perspex visor of Jade's helmet it looked like a bad dream – but one that was strangely familiar.

An old, ugly dream that had haunted her childhood.

The bike entered a long driveway with speed bumps and buildings on either side, buildings that looked like a cross between prison blocks and hospital wards – which was exactly what they were. For this was a prison hospital for some of the most dangerous criminals in the world – people who had committed crimes so terrible they were judged insane and locked up in this place for years and years, in some cases for ever. Jade sensed them watching her through the dark windows, welcoming her to their world; a world of nightmares.

Is this what Aunt Em meant by *somewhere safe*?

They cruised on past the silent, sombre buildings, seeing no one, hearing nothing beside the low growl of the engine. It was curiously rural. There were landscaped terraces and cultivated farmland and playing fields with goalposts and a running track. The fields looked sodden and bleak. Rain spattered on the visor of her helmet. And ahead was another fence with a single white building beyond. A prison within a prison.

They stopped at the entrance and Barney showed them his pass – the pass that seemed to open all doors – and the guards waved them through.

A long, single-storey building that looked like a temporary office block. Flowerbeds on each side of the door with a few evergreen shrubs that had obviously been there for some time. And a car park – with a handful of cars parked in the numbered bays. Barney stopped the bike next to one of them and helped her take off the helmet.

The building didn't look any better without the dark filter. There were a couple of lights on but otherwise it seemed empty. She noticed a tall, thin chimney at the far end. For burning what? A flurry of bitter rain stung her cheeks.

'What've you brought me here for?' she said. It was almost a whisper.

'To meet your Aunt Emily,' he said.

Two people were waiting for her in the lobby. Neither of them was Aunt Em.

'Jade, isn't it? How are you feeling?' A man in a white coat, quite old, smiling, kindly. 'Had a bit of a shock, I suppose. Never mind, soon have you right.'

His voice sounded too loud for the space they were in. There was no one on the reception desk.

'Please to sit.' A woman, also in a white coat, pushing a wheelchair. Not so kindly, her accent harsh and foreign.

'In the wheelchair?'

'Just in case,' said the man, still smiling.

In case of what, Jade wondered? What did they think was wrong with her? She sat gingerly in the wheelchair and the woman wheeled her along an empty corridor and into a room that looked like a doctor's surgery.

'Now then, let's have a look at you,' said the man in the white coat – presumably a doctor.

He shone a light in her eyes and tested her for double vision and did some other things that didn't make much sense to Jade but which she endured without complaint until he said, 'Well, no problems there that I can see.'

Had they got her mixed up with someone else?

'So can I go home now?' she said.

This seemed to take him back a bit.

'Home?' he said. It seemed to be a strange concept to him. He frowned and pressed his lips together thoughtfully. 'Ah well, I think we have to wait for Dr Mortlake to give her opinion on that.'

It took a moment or two to remember that 'Dr Mortlake' was Aunt Em.

'But I'll tell you what,' he said cheerfully, 'you just stay with the nurse here and I'll be back in a minute.' And with that he practically fled from the room.

Jade looked at 'the nurse here'. She smiled but it looked like it took an effort and the smile didn't come anywhere near reaching her eyes. Somehow, even without reading her mind, Jade knew this was not a woman who was comfortable with children. Or people generally. She looked about thirty-something with hair so short she was almost bald, and a round, shiny face that looked as if it had just been scrubbed . . . and cold, blue eyes. She reminded Jade of someone, but for the moment she couldn't think who. There was something not quite right about her, something artificial. A cold fish. It was an expression her mother used and it suited her perfectly.

She had a small scar on her upper lip, probably where the hook had caught her, and after the attempt at a smile she folded her hands primly in her lap and stared at the wall.

Jade found a different piece of wall to stare at. But she was thinking hard. She still had her phone in her jacket pocket but what would the woman do if she tried to use it? Jade decided not to take the risk. Better to save it for when she was alone. If they ever left her alone.

Then the door opened and Aunt Em walked in.

'Hello, you,' she said. 'You forgot your hat.'

And she threw Jade's cap across the room so that it landed in her lap. She stared at it and then at Aunt Em and felt like bursting into tears – or running across the room and hugging her.

But Jade didn't do bursting into tears and Aunt Em didn't do hugs – she went all stiff and awkward and patted you on the head — so Jade just sat there and did nothing.

'I guess you're wondering what's going on,' said Aunt Em regarding her with a frown, as if she was the main problem.

They were sitting in her office just along the corridor from the doctor's surgery. It was only a small office but Jade had an idea that Aunt Em pretty well ran the show — whatever the show was. Certainly the people in the white coats seemed to think so. *We have to wait for Dr Mortlake to give her opinion on that.*

She wondered where to begin. Probably with the men in masks.

'Who . . . ?' she began.

But Aunt Em was already shaking her head.

'Don't know,' she said. 'They drove off as soon as you'd gone.'

'So . . . ?'

'So I guess we have to assume it was you they were after. That's why I thought it best to bring you here.'

'But why would they be after me? What . . .'

Aunt Em held her hand up like a weary policeman stopping traffic. 'All in good time.'

All in good time?

Was she mad? And that was another thing . . .

'And why are we in Houndwood?'

'It's where I work. One of the places anyway. And it's not really Houndwood. It's the Annex.'

Oh, *the Annex*, oh well, that's all right then.

'But why didn't we go home and phone the police?'

Aunt Em gnawed a bit at her bottom lip. Then she said: 'Look, Jade, I know you have a lot of questions and you deserve the answers. I'll try to give you them but . . . you'll have to bear with me for a while.'

She stood up, walked over to the window and peered through the blinds. She hadn't put the light on and they were sitting in the gloom. It was still raining. At least there were no bars on the windows.

'You spoke to your mother?'

'Yes, but . . .'

'And she told you they were on their way?'

'Yes, but . . .'

'The thing is, before they get here there's something I've got to tell you.' She turned round and her face seemed very pale in the half-light. Jade thought she looked nervous. 'That is, something they've asked me to explain to you. Something important. Only it's a bit difficult. In fact it's very difficult.'

Jade had never seen her looking so unsure of

herself. She looked frightened. She looked *trapped*. Suddenly Jade's stomach was full of butterflies. Or moths. Or bats. Or all three and a few things besides that were considerably worse.

'Something to do with me?'

Aunt Em came and sat down on the chair next to her, on the same side of the desk.

'Where to begin?' she said with a sigh. She sat collecting her thoughts and when she began it was like a story and for a moment Jade thought it wasn't gong to be about her at all.

'Some years ago, before you were born, a man was sent to Houndwood – as a patient. His name was Dr Kobal and he was a scientist, a geneticist like me. He was a brilliant man but also, I'm afraid, quite mad. The original mad scientist. Mad and bad and dangerous to know . . .'

She seemed to drift off into her own thoughts. Jade waited impatiently. It would be so much quicker she thought, just to read people's minds. It would save so much time and energy and they wouldn't be able to lie, or hide things from you. If only it wasn't for the migraines.

'But his work was very important,' Aunt Em went on. 'It could have saved many lives and so it was

120

decided, at a very high level, that he should be allowed to continue his work here, under careful supervision. And so they built the Annex and moved in a team of researchers to assist him. One of whom was me.'

'What kind of work?' Jade thought of all the mad scientists she had seen in horror films on television – and the monsters they had made.

Aunt Em looked at her helplessly for a moment. Then she brightened and said: 'Hang on a minute. I've got to go fetch something. Be right back.'

Then she fled from the room.

Jade sat there a moment feeling nervous. What on earth was she going to bring back with her?

She stood up and crossed over to the window where Aunt Em had been standing. She half expected to see her father's Ford Focus rolling up but the car park was as bleak and miserable as it had been when she had arrived with Barney the Biker. That was another question she wanted to ask. What part did he have to play in all of this? But it was way down the list.

The rain seemed to have set in for what was left of the day, a chill winter drizzle that made you wish you could run away. Sneak aboard one of those planes at Heathrow and fly off to some distant country where there were blue skies and blue seas and white surf and palm trees and where you could be whoever you wanted to be. And never have to face up to who you really were.

Aunt Em came back. She was carrying a small metal dish and a box of eggs.

'This,' she said, 'is a Petri dish.' She put it on the table and took an egg out of the egg box. 'And this is an egg. A hen's egg.'

Was this for real?

She cracked the egg on the side of the Petri dish and Jade looked at the little pool of yellow yolk floating in the white.

'Now if this egg was fertilized by the rooster, it would hatch out into a little chicken.'

'Not now it wouldn't,' said Jade. 'Not after what you've done to it.'

'All right, smarty pants . . .' This was what teachers like Miss Simpson meant when they said Jade was too clever by half. 'But just imagine we injected the egg with things that made the chicken bigger and stronger and healthier. What would you think of that?'

Jade shrugged. Big, strong, healthy chickens were all very well if you liked that kind of thing but she wasn't going to get too excited about them.

'We could make it grow up with more meat and less fat. Or grow up more quickly. We could even make it a different colour. If there was a demand for it.'

She took a deep breath and Jade knew she was finally getting to the point.

'And some people think you can do the same with human eggs. You can change the genetic structure and grow a perfect baby – the baby you always wanted – either a girl or a boy with your dad's hair and your mom's eyes, and maybe somebody else's nose, because maybe Mom and Dad have big noses . . . A baby who will grow up beautiful and intelligent and athletic and . . . everything you want. A perfect designer baby.'

Just as horrifying as a monster, in its way . . .

'And that's what . . .' she started to say.

'No. No. Definitely not. That is not what we were doing. No way.'

She seemed quite sure about that then.

'It isn't allowed. Not in this country. Nor in most countries in the world. There are dangers. The science is in its infancy. No one knows how it might . . . And besides, there are moral questions, ethical questions . . . People talk about playing God. You can't even choose the sex of your baby. Not legally.

No, our work – Dr Kobal's work – was strictly limited by the law. We only used eggs that hadn't been fertilized. Eggs donated for medical research. Eggs that couldn't develop into . . . human beings. And our research was specifically into inherited diseases. How to isolate them – and get rid of them. That was all. Anything else was strictly off limits. But . . .' She sighed and pressed her fingers against her forehead as if she had a migraine coming on. 'Unfortunately the supervision wasn't careful enough – or Dr Kobal was too clever for us, too *mad* – and, in short, it was discovered that he had been doing some research of his own. Research into producing what you might call designer babies. But by the time this was discovered Dr Kobal had fled. Escaped. Taking his eggs with him. Frozen and stored in liquid nitrogen. All but one.'

Jade stared at her. Then she stared at the broken egg in the Petri dish and started to feel sick.

'What happened to it?' It was almost a whisper.

'Well, about a month after Dr Kobal escaped, one of the women patients was found to be pregnant. The men and women are kept in separate wings – it would have been impossible for them to get together – but just before he was found out Dr Kobal had treated her for something — it was most irregular but . . . it happened. And she became pregnant. Of course it might have happened in a more natural way but . . . we think Dr Kobal paid her a lot of money — I mean, there was a hefty sum went into her bank account — he was a very rich man — and a fertilized egg was planted in her uterus. And she insisted on having the baby. There were complications and she went into one of the local maternity hospitals. But security was a bit lax and soon after the birth she disappeared.'

'And the baby . . . ?' Jade's voice didn't sound like her own.

'The baby was a normal, healthy baby. A lovely baby. And she grew into a normal, healthy child. A lovely child.'

She was looking directly at Jade now. But Jade looked away. There was a terrible emptiness inside her. Like her insides had been vacuumed out.

'Me.'

'You.'

She reached out and squeezed Jade's hand. But it would have taken more than that to get rid of the emptiness.

'So that woman was my mother?'

'Not your natural mother. At least we don't think so. We call her the surrogate.' She sounded relieved to be talking technicalities again.

'Because you didn't have a natural mother – or father – you were made a ward of court. That means the courts became your legal guardians. They appointed me – because of my medical knowledge – as your kind of . . . supervisor. And your mom and dad – I mean, the people you've always thought of as your mom and dad – they were appointed to be your foster parents. And they are your proper mom and dad in every way, don't you think?'

But Jade didn't want to think about it. Not now. Probably not ever.

'What about Dr Kobal?' she said.

'Oh, well, about two years later he was tracked down to the US where he was running a clinic. He was arrested but, well, he had good lawyers and there was some problem over proving his identity, and to cut a long story short he was released on bail and he did a runner – and he's been running ever since.'

'And now you think he might be after me.'

'Well . . . yes.'

'Great,' said Jade flatly.

Well, she'd always wanted to be someone special.

'Lately I've had a sense I was being watched . . .' began Aunt Em.

Tell me about it, thought Jade.

'And I figured it was something to do with you. Someone was trying to find out where you were and reckoned that sooner or later I was going to lead them to you. So I had some of my own people watch my back. Barney's one of them. Just as well he was there, hey?'

'But why bring me here?'

'I just thought it would be safe. Secure. And there's not many people working here on Saturdays so . . . well, I've got an office here so I thought we could talk.'

'You should have told me. You should have told me earlier. Not waited till now.'

Aunt Em looked uncomfortable. 'I know but . . . we were just waiting for the right time. Your mom had discussed it with me. She thought it was getting close.'

Jade remembered hearing her on the phone.

It's happening. I think it's time.

She looked round the tiny office. Suddenly she felt angry. Anger was the one emotion she felt she could handle at the moment.

'So what do you *do* here? Do you still make babies?'

'No, Jade, we don't make babies. We never made babies. At least we never intended to. No, we try to put right the mess that Dr Kobal made . . .'

She realized what she had said.

'I didn't mean that. Oh, Jade . . .' But then her mobile phone rang. She fished it out of her handbag and listened for a moment. Then she said: 'I have to take this, do you mind?'

She left the room and closed the door behind her.

Jade was left alone with her anger. She felt angry about many, many things, but most of all with her parents, for not being her parents, and for not telling her until now.

But of course they *hadn't* told her, not even now. They'd left that to Aunt Em. Why? Because of the science? Because they thought she might have problems understanding it? She lashed out at the Petri dish and sent it flying across the room. The egg spattered on the wall and dripped slowly down on to the floor.

She stared at the mess in horror, thinking of the trouble she'd get into. Then she thought, No, I won't. They wouldn't dare. I'll never be in trouble ever again – not with *them*. And besides – *I won't be here.*

She made her mind up in that moment. She wasn't going to be here when they arrived.

She crossed over to the window again. It was almost dark now. The floodlights were on all along the perimeter fence. How could she get out past the men on the gate? Even then she'd still be in the hospital grounds with at least one other gate to get through before she reached the outside world.

She drew sharply back as someone came out of the building. Not that there was much chance of seeing her, standing there in the gloom.

It was the nurse who'd been left to look after her before Aunt Em arrived. She was wearing a red shiny raincoat and a red plastic hat, with a red handbag slung over her shoulder. She looked more doll-like than ever; like a doll dressed up for going out in the rain. She was heading for one of the parked cars. As she approached it she pointed the key to unlock the doors and the lights flashed on the car.

Jade had an idea. She stared hard at her through the window.

The keys, she thought, *where are my keys?*

The woman abruptly stopped and stared at the key in her hand.

The house keys, Jade beamed at her urgently. *I left them on the desk.*

She saw the woman thinking about it. Part of her mind knew the keys were in her handbag but Jade concentrated on the other part that said they were on her desk. It was only a small part, like a little seed that Jade had planted there, but she concentrated on making it grow and grow until it took over her whole mind.

The woman looked around sharply, and for a moment she seemed to be staring straight at Jade through the half-open blinds, but then she turned round and walked back into the building.

Within seconds Jade had opened the window and climbed out. Her first instinct was to run towards the car but forced herself to walk calmly over so that if anyone saw her on the CCTV they would think nothing of it. She threw a brief glance back towards the building. No one in sight. Then she opened the car door and lay down on the floor between the front and back seats.

Moments later she heard the woman get in and start the engine.

12

The Demons on the Roof

Brother Benedict peered through the cabin window as the aircraft dropped through the dirty, darkening skies above Heathrow Airport. The captain had said the temperature was two degrees Celsius and that it was raining. Welcome to England.

Somewhere in the murk below was the village of Rackthorne and the neighbouring complex of Houndwood Hospital. Benedict had identified them on the map on his laptop computer before he had been told to switch it off for the landing. Houndwood was, of course, known to him – he had even known a few of its patients over the years – but he had *not* known, until he had read it on the computer, that it had once been in the middle of a forest – and that pockets of it still remained in the area.

He was aware of the possible significance of this.

From the case of his laptop he took out a small notebook and riffled through the pages until he found the drawing of a star. A large seven-pointed star or septagram, known to those who dabbled in the occult as the elven or fairy star. In the drawing each of the points had been given a name: Sun, Forest, Sea, Magic, Moon, Wind and Spirit. Now, next to the word 'Forest' Benedict wrote Piru and under that Rackthorne, with a question mark.

Rackthorne. The place in the forest where three paths meet.

Piru. The demons of the forest.

He was a man who believed in symbols – and codes – and the use to which they could be put by his enemies. There was a code here if only he could crack it. But too much remained a mystery to him. He needed more information.

There was a strange rumbling noise and the plane seemed to judder in the air. Benedict knew it was probably just the wheels being lowered but he gripped both sides of his seat and closed his eyes. He hated flying. It felt unnatural, a defiance of the laws of gravity. He was aware that this might be thought ironic in one of his background and lineage.

It was dark by the time he came out of the terminal – and raining hard. He had to make a dash for the Oxford coach and the driver grumbled at having to open up the luggage compartment again and take his 'skis'. There were only a few passengers and he found a window seat and phoned the college to tell them to expect him for supper. Then he pulled up the hood of his leather jacket and settled down to sleep through most of the journey down the rain-lashed motorway.

The coach dropped him within a short walk of the college but the High Street gate was closed and he had to walk through the dark, dingy passage to the side entrance. He had his head down and his hood up with his skis over his shoulder, and he didn't see the two figures until he almost walked into them. Like him, they both wore hoods and at first he took them for students but then he suddenly found himself pinned against the wall with a knife pressed to his throat.

The skis had crashed to the ground but he kept hold of the shoulder bag.

'What do you want?' he said.

'What have you got?' said the one with the knife.

Benedict could smell stale breath and cigarettes. He was just a kid, about eighteen or nineteen. Probably not a student, though you never could tell. He glanced back the way he had come. He could see the lights of the High Street at the end of the passage but it might as well have been a mile away.

'I've got about two hundred pounds in my wallet,' he said. 'Will that do you?'

The youth told him to get it out and not try anything.

Benedict pulled out his wallet but before he could take out the money the youth snatched it from his hand. Benedict tried to think if there was anything in the wallet he would really mind losing and decided there was not. But then the other youth made a grab for the shoulder bag.

Benedict hung on to it.

'Look,' he said calmly. 'You can have the wallet but I'm afraid I can't let you have the bag or the skis. Sorry.'

He was looking into the eyes of the boy with the knife but he didn't know his companion was similarly armed until he felt a thump in his right side that drove the air out of his lungs. He looked down and saw the hilt sticking out of his ribs.

He dropped the bag to the ground.

'Do you have no idea of the value of human life?' he said.

The boy stared at him as if he was mad. He pulled the knife out and Benedict felt a gush of warm blood down his side and an excruciating pain.

The first boy had stood back but now, possibly feeling he had to compete, he lunged at Benedict's face.

But Benedict was no longer there.

He moved so fast it was impossible to see quite how he did it but the knife smashed into the wall and the boy found his wrist held in an iron grip and jerked sharply upwards. In the same movement Benedict stepped under it and turned, twisting it behind his assailant's back.

The boy cried out in pain and the knife fell clattering to the floor.

That would normally have been enough for Benedict but because he was angry he pressed his left hand against the back of the boy's head and cracked it hard against the wall.

He let him drop and turned to see what the other

thug was doing. He was already coming at him, swearing and slashing at his face with the knife. Benedict twisted sideways, knocked the blade aside with his left hand and chopped the edge of his right hand sharply into the carotid nerve on the side of the boy's neck.

The shock of the blow travelled right down the boy's arm and the knife flew from his grasp.

Benedict stepped back a little to give himself some distance and then drove his forearm into the boy's nose.

He fell on his knees with his hands to his face, blood spurting between his fingers. He made a sound like a small animal caught in a trap.

Benedict looked inside his jacket. There was a jagged tear and a dark patch of blood on his T-shirt but the bleeding had almost stopped. He pressed the edges of the wound together with a finger and thumb and held them for a moment. Then he gathered up the knives and rammed them into the wall, one after the other, with a force that snapped the blades at the hilt.

Then he took both youths by the collar and half dragged, half carried them round to the front of the building.

He lifted their heads up so they could see the gargoyles on the roof. Some of them were old acquaintances; others he did not know so well. There was Dragnignazzo, the fell dragon, Ciriato Sonnutu, the tusked boar and Caynazzo, the snarler. None of them particularly reliable — barely a brain cell between the three of them — but they would do for his purpose.

He formed a mental picture and projected it into the minds of the two youths.

After a moment one of them began to make moaning noises and covered his eyes. The other just stared in horror with his mouth open.

Benedict knew what they could see.

They could see two of the gargoyles sliding down the roof like lizards moving on two juicy moths. Large lizards with outsize heads. Caynazzo had started to dribble rather disgustingly from his mouth.

So had one of the youths. The other seemed to have fainted.

Benedict shook him till he opened his eyes.

'See that,' he said.

It was apparent that they did.

Benedict froze the image just before the demons reached the ground.

The two youths were now struggling desperately but Benedict held on to them with no apparent effort.

'They know you now,' he said. 'And they know where to find you if you ever do anything like this again. And believe me, you don't want that to happen. Do you understand me?'

He took it that they did.

He dropped them to the ground.

'Now go, my sons,' he said, reverently making the sign of the cross, 'and sin no more.'

They picked themselves up and fled down the High Street.

Benedict shook his head over the tear in the side of his leather jacket and then went back up the passage to recover his things.

'Welcome back, sir,' said the porter when he stepped into the lodge. 'Been skiing? How was the snow?'

'Not bad for the time of year, thank you, John,' said Benedict. 'How's yourself?'

He found Professor Higgins in his rooms.

'Good Lord,' said the professor, recoiling a pace. 'Look what the cat's brought in.'

Brother Benedict, who had changed into a suit and a clean shirt, thought this a little harsh. Especially coming from one who looked as if he was dressed in sackcloth and ashes and whose gaunt but striking features were framed by a wild mass of grey hair and beard. Indeed, if anyone had been asked to guess which of these two was the monk he would not have paused a second before indicating the distinguished professor.

'I heard there was cottage pie for supper,' Benedict said, 'and jam roly-poly to follow. How could I resist?'

'I thought you were a vegetarian. Anyway, come in, and have a drink. Unless you've given it up.'

Benedict assured him that he hadn't and Prof Higgins found a very good bottle of malt whisky and poured generously for both of them.

'Well, it's very good of you to drop in, dear boy,' he said. 'I must say I'd given up all hope of you in this life.'

'If you think there's the faintest chance of meeting in the next,' Benedict assured him, 'you can have no idea what the rules are like.'

He sank down in one of the ancient leather armchairs with a sigh of relief. If he thought of anywhere as home it was All Souls College and this was one of his favourite rooms.

He glanced around the walls of books, some of

which even he had not read, reassuring himself that nothing had changed since his last visit. There were probably a few more books but otherwise all was as it should be. He noted with approved the medieval carvings of the Pardoner and the Wife of Bath from the Canterbury Tales with their worn features and faded colours; the bronze sculpture of the Templar Knight with his pilgrim's staff instead of a sword; and the painting on the wall above the fireplace: an unusual study of Venice without the canals by Francesco Guardi showing the church of San Francesco della Vigna in the Campo – one of Benedict's favourites.

If only he could stay here for a millennium or so and let the world go by.

But even the professor did not have that luxury. Though he looked such a fossil – and had a passion for the Middle Ages – he was very closely tuned to the modern world. His profession was criminology and he was often called in to advise police and government on his specialist subject – the detection of method in madness.

'So, what is your particular quest at this present moment in time?' the professor quizzed him. 'A fell dragon? A demon from the darkest depths of Hell?

The seventh seal? The holy grail? Or the new barmaid at the Eagle and Child.'

Benedict raised an eyebrow.

'*Is* there a new barmaid at the Eagle and Child?'

'Brygida. Polish lass. Make a monk forsake his vows. Fancy a pint in the snug?'

'Maybe later,' Benedict said. 'At the moment I have other concerns. How long is it since you were last in Houndwood Hospital?'

13

Escape from Houndwood

Jade could tell from the blaze of light that they were approaching the security gates. She made herself as small as possible in the space between the seats but anyone glancing through the rear window could hardly fail to see her.

The car stopped. She heard the whirr of the front window being lowered and the approach of footsteps.

A man's voice – presumably a security guard – and the woman's brief reply.

Then they were through.

But only into the grounds of the hospital.

The real test would come when they reached the outer gates – the gates that led to freedom and where the guards would be much more thorough. Her only chance was if they thought she was a coat that had dropped on to the floor.

Maybe she could *think* them into *thinking* she was a coat.

If she could think her teacher into seeing bats and the nurse into thinking she'd left her keys behind it had to be worth a try . . .

The car came to a halt. It was dark so they couldn't have reached the security gates. She lay still as a mouse. Or a coat.

'I think is better you sit in front.'

Jade didn't move.

'Hey, you in back, you hear what I say? If you stay there they see you. They want know why you lie on floor.'

Slowly Jade scrambled up on to the seat. She met the woman's eyes in the rear-view mirror. Cold, unblinking eyes. Like a cat's watching a mouse or a small bird.

'Can you climb over or you want I open the door?'

'I can climb over,' said Jade. Her mysterious powers clearly had their limits.

She squirmed between the two front seats.

'How did you know I was there?'

'I see you from inside. Fasten your seat belt.'

They drove on. But not back to the Annex.

Jade could see the main gates ahead in a glare of floodlights.

'Give me your pass,' said the nurse.

Jade realized she was still wearing the visitor's pass they had given her on the way in. She unclipped it from her jacket and passed it over.

Was she going to hand her in?

'You let me do talking, OK? You say nothing.'

So she sat there, saying nothing, while the nurse did the talking.

'Who's this?' said the guard.

'Dr Mortlake's niece,' said the nurse. 'I'm taking her home.'

Now was the time to speak, if she was going to speak.

The guard checked a list on a clipboard and ticked it. Then he looked in the back of the car and checked the boot.

Then he waved them through.

Jade didn't know whether to be sorry or relieved. A small but insistent voice, very like Aunt Em's, told her that she was being extremely foolish. She ignored it. She was still very angry with Aunt Em – *and* her so-called parents. Let them sweat.

'Why are you helping me?' she asked as they

pulled away from the gate.

'I take pity on you.'

'Uh huh.' Somehow Jade doubted it. Not with those eyes. 'So where are you taking me?'

'Where you want go?'

Silence.

'Well, when you know, maybe you tell me.'

Where *could* she go? Her school friends might help but they all lived with their parents and she knew what *they'd* do. But with her own parents on their way here the house would be empty. She could let herself in and pick up a few things. She had some money in her room. Just over forty-five pounds from her last birthday. She imagined catching a train and going as far as she could. She'd always wanted to travel through the night on a train. Or she could pick up her passport and leave the country. She could go anywhere she liked. For up to forty-five pounds.

A pair of headlights swept towards them and she caught a glimpse of the oncoming car. She ducked down in her seat until it passed by.

'Why you do that?' said the nurse.

'My parents,' Jade whispered, as if they could hear her.

Maybe she should start thinking of them as her

foster parents. She needed time to sort out how she felt about all this and what, if anything, she could do about it.

She twisted round to look back and saw the car stop at the security barrier. They'd soon find out she wasn't there. If Aunt Em hadn't found out already.

Suddenly she heard a familiar blast of music. In the excitement of her escape she'd completely forgotten about her mobile phone. She fished it out of her pocket and flipped the cover.

A hand reached out and snatched it from her.

Jade stared at her in alarm.

'What you doing?' she demanded.

'Better not to answer.'

She dropped it into the side pocket of the door.

For the first time Jade felt really scared. The stuff with the men in masks had happened so fast she hadn't had the chance to feel anything much, except a buzz of adrenalin. But this was something else. She was completely in this woman's power and there was precious little she could do about it.

'So you know where you want to go yet?'

'I'd like to go home.' She tried to sound firm. 'But you can just drop me off at a station if you like.'

They were driving through the village of

Rackthorne. If they slowed down at a crossroads maybe she could jump out. She felt furtively for the door handle.

An eerie wailing noise, rising and falling . . . like something she'd heard in a movie, at the start of an air raid.

The sirens!

They rang them whenever someone escaped from Houndwood. The police would be setting up roadblocks. They'd stop the car and find her.

But they were practically out of the village, the sound of the sirens fading into the distance. All she could hear was the swish of the windscreen wipers and the hiss of the tyres on the wet road. The headlights carved a path through the murky night. Hedgerows on either side . . .

Then – on the road ahead – a flashing blue light.

The car skidded to a halt. But the woman's hand was already on the gear lever, slamming it into reverse.

'What you doing?' Jade yelled as they careered back down the dark road.

But then she braked again and in the headlights Jade saw a narrow gap in the hedge.

'No!' she yelled and raised her hands to her face as the woman drove straight for it. A thump, a sickening lurch, branches scouring the windows and they were through and hurtling down a track through fields. They plunged into a large puddle. Mud swamped the windscreen.

'Where you taking us?' Jade shouted.

'Short cut,' said the woman and laughed. Not a pleasant laugh. A kind of madness in it. Then she switched off the lights.

It was pitch black. The woman slowed down a little and hit the screen washer. When the mud cleared Jade saw a wood ahead, the trees stark and grim against the night sky. She switched the headlights on again. There was a wide path – or a firebreak – running through the middle of the wood. They raced down it as if they were in a tunnel, the gaunt trees rushing past on either side. Something leaped in front of them. A deer – frozen in the glare of the headlights. Jade screamed. Then it was gone.

And they were out of the wood and on a winding country lane.

They followed it for several miles. No other cars. Not even a house. Then lights ahead and suddenly they were on a main road in heavy traffic. And a blue illuminated sign that said 'London 17 miles'.

Jade breathed a small sigh of relief. Maybe they

were going home. Another blast of music. The woman clamped a phone – not Jade's – to her ear. She listened for a moment and then said: 'I call you back.'

They pulled into a lay-by and she got out and walked a short distance from the car and started talking on the phone – but her eyes stayed on Jade.

Who was she talking to? What was she thinking?

Jade concentrated but it didn't work. Almost immediately she felt the beginning of a migraine. She couldn't handle another migraine. Not now.

She wondered if she could make a run for it. She watched the woman tensely as she spoke on the phone, her free hand beating the air for emphasis. But she was no longer looking towards the car.

Jade leaned over the driver's seat and made a dive for her phone.

But it wasn't there.

The door opened.

The woman shook her finger warningly.

'Was that my Aunt Em?' Jade asked her.

'You think I do this to give you back Dr Mortlake?'

Jade didn't think that. But why *was* she doing it?

They drove on. After a little while they turned off the main road again on to another country lane. Forest on either side. Jade's heart was pounding.

'Why did you turn off?' she said.

'Because the police have number of car. Is better we stick to back road.'

But after a few minutes she swung off into a car park. Picnic tables in the headlights, a ring of trees. She stopped and switched off the lights.

It was very dark.

Jade was seriously scared. This was the nightmare she'd always feared; the situation she'd always been warned against.

But she was with a woman. A nurse. Surely there was nothing to fear from a nurse.

'Why have we stopped?' she demanded.

'We wait.'

'What for?'

But the woman closed her eyes and put her head back against the headrest. After a few minutes with no sound, no movement, Jade quietly released her seat belt and groped for the door handle. She'd barely touched it when the voice said calmly and with a trace of boredom: 'What are you doing?'

'I . . . I just thought I'd . . . I'd get out for a minute.'

'Is better you stay here.' She didn't bother to open her eyes.

Jade sat staring through the mud-spattered window at the lonely, silent woods. The pale tree trunks faded into a menacing darkness. It had stopped raining but drips fell on the car roof and a thin mist hung in the upper branches. She could hear the noise of some night bird, an owl perhaps. And then suddenly there was a fox. It stood on the edge of the clearing, staring at the car. Then, after a moment, two cubs appeared and started clowning around, making little runs at each other, biting and pawing. Then they stood on their hind legs and started to box. Jade knew she was seeing something very special, almost magical, but she was too scared to appreciate it.

Suddenly the foxes stopped and stared at something beyond the parked vehicle, back towards the road. And in a blink they were gone.

Moments later Jade heard the sound of a car engine. Headlights swept across the trees and a car turned off the road and drove slowly towards them. The lights dipped and dimmed and the engine was switched off.

The door opened and a man got out.

14

The Last Monk

Benedict woke with a start. It was pitch black and for a moment he could not think where he was. He groped for the light switch and sat up in bed. He was in his own room, high in the roof of All Souls College. A small room, almost a monk's cell and as simply furnished.

He had been dreaming. A nightmare. He tried to remember the details. There was a forest in it somewhere and some animals and a child. *The* child? Then a bright light in his eyes and a figure framed in a door, advancing towards him . . .

And then he had woken up.

He picked up his watch from the bedside table and focused on the time. Ten past seven. He swung his feet out of bed, shivering in the cold, and padded to the window to twitch back the curtain.

Dark and foggy. A November fog, so thick he could barely see the buildings on the opposite side of the quad. The modern world was erased. Masked and muffled. It might have been the winter he first came here and he would have been preparing to join his brother monks in the chapel for morning prayers. Forty scholars, hand-picked by the archbishop, to serve the highest offices of Church and State. And to pray for the souls of the faithful departed.

But he was the only monk here now – the last monk of All Souls – and he had different duties.

The skis were propped against the wall. He unzipped the bag and reassembled the rifle. He checked the firing mechanism and added a drop of oil from a small can in the toolbox. Then he opened the wardrobe and pulled out a long canvas holdall containing a fishing rod with a pair of reels and several boxes for flies and bait. When he took them out there was plenty of room for both the rifle and the telescopic sights. He put the remaining bullets in the metal bait box, still filled with sawdust for the maggots. Then he dressed and groped his way down the winding staircase and out into the quad.

It was cold and dank. He could have been in a bog. Lights glimmered like jack-o-lanterns, the ghostly sprites that lured unwary travellers to their death. He heard the distant sound of the Agnes Dei, the beautiful plainsong of the monks in the chapel. A dim echo of the past. but no, it was real. Probably from a CD in one of the rooms. Then the clatter of a saucepan in the kitchens. A faint smell of toast and coffee . . .

A figure lurched out of the mist towards him. It wore a long overcoat, a muffler wrapped round the lower part of the face and a woollen hat pulled low over the ears.

Benedict recognized the beetling brows and the hawk nose of Professor Higgins.

He seized Benedict's arm in a claw-like grip.

'I was coming to wake you,' he said. 'There's something on the news. About Houndwood – and a child.'

15

Cloud Cuckoo Land

Jade awoke. That is to say her eyes opened.

Wide. As if in shock.

Whether or not she was awake, or even alive, was another matter.

She was lying on a mattress on the floor. The room had no furniture and no carpet and the walls were concrete. It looked more like a garage than the room of a house. A garage . . . or a cell. And it was filled with a pale, unearthly light.

She had no idea where she was or how she came to be here.

This was scary. But not half as scary as the memory that came flooding back a moment later.

A clearing in a forest. Car headlights sweeping

towards her and stopping. The lights dimming and the door opening and the man stepping out. She wanted to scream or run. To scream *and* run. Not necessarily in that order. But she could do neither. She was like the deer caught in the car headlights.

The shattered pieces of a dream or something real?

She remembered groping for the handle of the car door and bracing herself for a swift dash into the forest. But someone had grabbed her arm. The woman – the nurse.

The nurse was real. She remembered her from the hospital.

And then the man was standing in the door looking down at her.

A tall man, quite young, with long dark hair. Wearing a black leather jacket and jeans. He spoke her name . . .

And then nothing.

Well, almost nothing. A hazy recollection of a journey through the night in the back of a car, dropping in and out of sleep. The headlights picking out trees. Wraiths of mist, drifting across the road. The man driving, the woman next to him.

But if there *had* been such a journey Jade had no

memory of how it had ended. Or how she came to be here in this bed, in this room.

For this was surely real.

She was in a sleeping bag. And there were her clothes, hanging on the back of the door and her boots neatly placed against the wall.

So what was she wearing?

She peered into the sleeping bag. A long, old-fashioned nightdress. It smelled freshly laundered.

She was conscious of a pain high up in her right arm. She pulled up her sleeve and craned her neck to inspect it. There was a red mark about halfway between her shoulder and her elbow. Was that where the woman had grabbed her? She had a memory of something sharp digging into her. One of her nails . . . or a needle?

She looked round the room again.

A door and a single small window with a piece of sacking over it and a pale light filtering through from the outside.

She wriggled out of the sleeping bag and padded over and looked out . . .

Nothing. She was in cloud.

Or fog.

She tried to open the window but it had a security

catch and no key. She pressed her face against the glass and made out dim shapes. Bushes or buildings? Or rocks? Hopeless. She turned away from the window and contemplated the door.

She approached it slowly, treading quietly on her bare feet. The concrete floor was very cold.

She turned the handle and gently pushed. Then pulled.

But it was locked.

She backed away and sat down on the bed. So it *was* a cell. And she was a prisoner.

A noise at the door.

She scrambled back into the sleeping bag and closed her eyes. A key turned in the lock and the door opened.

Jade squinted through one eye. The nurse, with a tray of food.

Jade suddenly felt terribly hungry. It was ages since she had last eaten. She had never gone so long without food in her life.

She acted as if she had just woken up.

The nurse put the tray down on the floor next to the mattress. There was orange juice and toast and jam and a boiled egg.

'Please to eat,' she said. 'And then to put clothes on.'

'Where am I?' Jade asked.

But the woman just said: 'Eat. And then put clothes on.'

Then she left the room and Jade heard the sound of a key turning in the lock.

She looked at the egg and remembered the one that Aunt Em had broken into the Petri dish. But even that couldn't put her off.

When she had finished breakfast she sat on the mattress for a few moments thinking things over. All this must have something to do with the circumstances of her birth. But what were they?

There had been an egg given by a donor. But what donor? And was the donor her *real* mother? The egg had been fertilized by a man. But what man? And was he her real father?

And then the egg had been planted in another woman. The surrogate. And nine months later Jade was born.

A perfectly natural lovely baby . . .

Was she?

'I don't think so,' she said aloud.

And she didn't think other people thought so either. Otherwise they wouldn't have been watching her so carefully.

She got dressed and went over to the window again. The fog was lifting. Not entirely but enough to see that it was rising from a lake. Or maybe the sea. But it seemed too calm for the sea. And there were reed beds. And then as the mist lifted a bit more she saw a boat at the end of a long jetty. A large yellow boat.

Except that it wasn't a boat. It was a plane. A yellow seaplane floating at the end of the jetty.

She'd never seen a seaplane before, not for real, only in books or on the Internet. As she stared, a gaggle of ducks swam up and gazed up at it as if it was some giant, much-improved version of themselves.

Someone at the door. The nurse again.

'Come,' she said. 'The doctor wish to speak with you.'

The doctor?

Warily Jade followed her down a long corridor with closed doors down one side and windows down the other, covered in sacking like the one in her room.

The woman unlocked the door at the end of the corridor and they entered what seemed to be a kind of warehouse or hangar. They walked across it, their footsteps echoing in the vast, empty space and through another door and into . . .

A jungle.

At least that was the first impression. Tall palm trees, exotic plants, vines and creepers, a blast of warm, damp air . . . and the sound of birds. Birds you didn't hear in England outside a zoo. Then she saw that it was a large conservatory. A thin steam seeped from pipes running around the walls and condensed on the windows and dripped on the floor. Within seconds Jade felt uncomfortably warm.

'Come,' said the woman, and Jade followed her through the palm trees and along the side of an ornamental pond filled with golden carp, and then up a spiral staircase to a kind of wrought-iron platform or deck, with a table laid for breakfast.

And sitting there, drinking coffee, was the man Jade had met the night before in the car park in the middle of the forest.

His long hair looked as if it had just been washed and combed out to dry. He wore an earring in one ear and a long flowing robe that Jade thought might be a Japanese kimono, gorgeously coloured. In fact he looked rather gorgeous himself and clearly knew it. Like Johnny Depp in *Pirates of the Caribbean* but without the beard and the eye make-up.

Who on earth was he?

'Hi, Jade,' he said airily, flapping a hand at her. 'Hope you slept well. Come and have some coffee. Do you drink coffee – or shall we get you some milk or something?'

He had an American accent, a bit like Aunt Em's.

Jade stared at him and despite her fears she felt her temper rising. She was fed up being mucked around with, manipulated, treated like a child.

'How dare you lock me into my room,' she said. 'Who do you think you are?'

He raised his eyebrows and looked mildly amused, and when he spoke again it was in a posh, obviously fake English accent.

'Do you know,' he said, 'I rather think I'm your father.'

16

The Fishing Trip

The professor had heard the news on the radio while he was still in bed but he had been half asleep at the time and didn't catch the name.

'They might not have given it,' he said. 'But I'm sure they said she came from Turnham Green. Of course it might be a coincidence.'

But Benedict was already heading for the common room in search of a television.

The story was the second lead on Teletext. Massive police hunt for missing girl. Eleven-year-old Jade Jarvis abducted from Houndwood Hospital where she had been visiting a member of staff.

Benedict sat down heavily. He looked very tired suddenly and old.

'Is it her?' said the professor.

Benedict didn't need to answer.

'If there's anything I can do to help . . .' the professor began.

Benedict rubbed a hand over his unshaven jaw.

'If it's who I think it is,' he said, 'he'll be trying to get her out of the country.'

'He? The police seem to think some woman is involved . . .'

'Even if she is,' said Benedict, 'she'll be working for Kobal.'

The professor had no idea who Kobal was and knew better than to ask. Brother Benedict was something of a legend at All Souls. He looked to be in his early thirties but some of the older Fellows claimed he had been here in their youth. He spent long periods away but his room was always kept ready for him. He was listed among the Distinguished Fellows but no one could remember when he was elected. And whenever anyone asked the Warden about him the Warden would just shrug and say: 'I think it's rather splendid for the college to have a monk in residence, don't you?' And that was the end of it.

But no one knew quite what kind of a monk he

was. He didn't seem to belong to any of the usual Christian orders and no one had ever seen him in the chapel praying.

The professor was probably closer to him than any of the other Fellows apart from the Warden himself. They had shared many an evening over a good bottle of claret or malt whisky in the professor's rooms discussing life's mysteries without ever touching on the mystery of Benedict himself.

But this was not something that particularly troubled the professor.

He was a man who loved mysteries. He loved solving them too but he knew you couldn't rush the process. A man who loves the dark knows better than to turn on the light.

So he simply said: 'They'll have a job getting her out of the country, whoever they are. The police will be keeping a tight watch on all the exit points.'

But Benedict was shaking his head.

'He won't take her out through any of the obvious channels,' he said. He seemed to be thinking aloud. 'He'll use a private plane. Or a boat.'

'It still won't be easy,' the professor insisted. 'You can't just come and go as you like. Not these days.'

Benedict looked at him thoughtfully. 'If you

wanted to fly a private plane out of the country – say across the North Sea – how would you go about it?'

'My dear fellow,' said the professor. 'I've really no idea. You'd have to ask a pilot.'

'What about the police? Wouldn't they know? You've got the best police contacts of anyone I know.'

'Well, I suppose I could give someone a ring,' the professor agreed doubtfully, looking at his watch. 'But it's a bit early.'

He was gone half an hour. When he came back he was clutching an envelope covered in notes and had the air of a man bulging with new-found information.

'Right,' he said, studying the envelope. 'All flights in and out of the UK – commercial and private – are monitored by Air Traffic Control. And the North Sea is covered by the control centre at Prestwick in Scotland.'

He shot a look at Benedict from under his bushy brows.

'I take it you are only interested in flights *out* of the country?'

The monk rolled his eyes.

'Very well. In the next twenty-four hours Prestwick have agreed flight plans for eleven private flights outbound across the North Sea. Seven of them are helicopters ferrying supplies or personnel to oil rigs. I take it we can discount them.'

'I think so, yes. Unless they're trying to smuggle her on to an oil rig.'

The professor ignored the sarcasm.

'Of the remaining four, three are executive jets to Norway and Denmark. Two from Newcastle. One from Edinburgh.'

'And the fourth?'

'A seaplane,' said the professor with quiet triumph. 'Flying from Orford Ness, in Suffolk.'

Benedict reached for the envelope but the professor held it from him and continued reading: 'Petrov Pez 202. Russian job, known in the UK as a Heron. Amphibian. That means it can land on land or water,' he explained helpfully. 'Arrived in Britain two days ago, on private business. Landed at Norwich Airport to clear customs and then flew on to Orford Ness, on the Suffolk coast, formerly a base for seaplanes of the Royal Navy Air Force.'

But Benedict was already halfway to the door.

'Where are you going?' the professor called after him.

'To hire a car,' Benedict threw back over his shoulder.

'No need for that.' The professor started after him. 'I'll drive you there.'

Benedict paused at the door.

'To Orford Ness?'

'To John o'Groats if you like.'

'You might be getting into something deep.'

'Good,' said the professor. 'I like deep. Just give me a few minutes to fetch the car.'

The professor's car was a 1972 Citroën DS – called by its French manufacturers the Déesse, or in plain English: the Goddess. It was his pride and joy but it had known better days. Benedict regarded it doubtfully.

'Are you sure it will get us there?' he demanded.

The professor was offended.

'Of course she'll get us there,' he declared indignantly. 'Provided the fog lifts and you don't hurt her feelings. She might be called the Goddess but she goes like the Devil.'

'And the Devil,' said Brother Benedict, 'is the father of lies.'

The professor snorted.

He noticed the bag slung over Benedict's shoulder.

'What's this?' he demanded. 'You planning on doing some fishing?'

'You never know,' Benedict replied. 'I always like to have the option.'

17

Dr Kobal

'My *father*?' Jade repeated incredulously.

'Father, dad, daddy . . .' Kobal had resumed his American accent. 'Pa, papa, old man . . .'

He spread his arms and began to sing:

'Oh mein papa, to me you are so wonderful . . .'

'Don't be stupid,' she interrupted him rudely. 'How can *you* be my father?'

He didn't seem at all put out.

'Well, I take it you understand the facts of life,' he said. 'Or do I have to explain them to you?'

'No, thank you,' she replied firmly.

'Well, what's the problem then?'

'What's the *problem*?'

She couldn't believe this.

'Sure. I mean, is there anything in particular you object to, or is it the general principle of the thing?'

'Well, for a start, you're not old enough.'

'That's very sweet of you but I promise you I am. A lot older than you think. Now will you please sit down because I find it kind of intimidating with you standing over me like that.'

Jade sat down. Not because he had told her to but because she felt a bit giddy all of a sudden. It might be the heat – or all these tropical plants draining the oxygen from the air. But then again it might be because twenty-four hours ago she had woken up in her bed in Turnham Green in the belief that her father was a short, fat, balding man with a ginger moustache who went by the name of James Francis Jarvis, and now she was expected to believe her real father was a young man with long dark hair and an earring, wearing a red and gold kimono, who went by the name of . . .

'Dr Kobal,' she said.

It came out a little breathlessly because it had just hit her that this was who he was.

If Aunt Em could be believed.

But then, how could she believe anything any more? She certainly couldn't believe anything her family told her. They weren't even her family. Her Aunt Em wasn't really her aunt; her mum and dad weren't really her mum and dad; a complete stranger was telling her he was her father . . . and she had a surrogate mother who had been a patient in a hospital for the criminally insane.

'I guess they told you I was mad.'

Mad, bad and dangerous to know . . .

'Well, they said you were in Houndwood . . .'

'And so I was. But I promise you I'm as sane as you are. And a lot saner than the people who put me there.'

She was too polite to argue. And too scared. The anger seemed to have evaporated in the heat – and the fear had returned . . . She was in the hands of a madman who had escaped from Houndwood.

Kobal stretched and the golden dragon on his kimono rippled alarmingly.

'I can see I had better tell you the whole story,' he said, 'but it will take a little time.'

He glanced out of the windows of the conservatory. From where they sat they had a fine view of the jetty with the yellow seaplane floating at the end. It seemed to have attracted a few more ducks. The fog was lifting but there was still a fair bit of it hanging around, especially over the water.

'However, as it doesn't look like we'll be going anywhere for a while.'

Where did he plan on going, she wondered, and did he plan to take her with him? A drip fell on her from the roof. She looked up and noticed a speaker in one of the trees. This seemed to be where the birdsong was coming from. She couldn't see any birds.

'What d'you think of the old den?' Dr Kobal asked her. 'I don't come here much and most of it's a bit kind of run-down nowadays but I like to keep the conservatory in shape. The birdsong's recorded, as I guess you realized. We had real birds once – parakeets – but they died. Some virus thing. I got a couple of gardeners come over from the mainland to look after the plants and tend to the boilers. I like a bit of warmth. It's a bit on the cold side where I live most of the time these days. But maybe it's a bit too warm for you. You like a cold drink? How about a beer?'

Jade stared at him.

'Is only child,' said a deep voice from behind them, 'the child they not drink the beer. For sure they not drink for breakfast.'

Jade turned to see the nurse sitting there with her arms folded at the far end of the platform. The jailer. She looked more like a doll than ever.

'They don't?' said Dr Kobal in surprise. 'But everyone drinks beer,' he added truculently. 'Beer and gruel. Regular British breakfast.'

'No more,' she said firmly. 'Only many years when water is bad, make ill. But now is OK and they make law you no more feed the child the beer.'

'You're kidding me.' Dr Kobal shook his head and frowned. 'Isn't that just typical of government?' he said to Jade.

Jade said nothing. Mad, she thought. The pair of them, the Mad Hatter and the March hare. Which probably made her Alice in Wonderland.

'Perhaps a rum and Coke?' Kobal suggested.

'I wouldn't mind some fruit juice,' said Jade coldly. 'If you have any.'

'Great.' He beamed. 'Perhaps Baer–Mellor would be kind enough to fetch you some.'

Jade wondered if she was hearing things.

'What did you just say?' she demanded.

'I said perhaps Baer–Mellor would be kind enough . . .'

'Barmella? Her name's Barmella?'

Kobal looked at her in surprise and then at the retreating figure of the nurse.

'Her full name is Sophie Caroline Maria Baer-Mellor von Koffen,' he said, 'but I find that a bit of a mouthful so I call her Baer-Mellor.' He frowned. 'I suppose I could call her Sophie but it would be a bit intimate, don't you think? She's a countess, you know.'

'I used to have a doll called Barmella,' said Jade faintly. 'I used to throw her against the wall.'

More than that. She'd even buried her once, in the back garden; a full-scale funeral with all the other dolls and animals as mourners. But later she'd dug her up and put her in the washing machine. She was on the wicker chair with all the other dolls – at least, Jade thought she was; a particularly ugly rag doll with a shiny round plastic face but no hair – and a dent in her forehead.

'What a very badly brought-up young lady you must have been,' remarked Kobal drily.

'But how could I have *done* that?'

'I expect it's your Aunt Em's influence. She always had a violent streak.'

'I mean, the name. It's not exactly common is it? It's not like calling her Britney or Kylie.'

Kobal looked puzzled. 'Who's Britney and Kylie, should I know them?'

Jade stamped her foot; something she hadn't done since she was about seven.

'I mean, why did I think of calling my doll Barmella?' she almost shrieked at him. 'Years before I met the real one.'

'Ah,' he said. 'Well perhaps that has something to do with the story I'm about to tell you.'

18

The Devil's Mirror

'I once had a brother,' began Dr Kobal, 'who was born with a dreadful handicap. It was dreadful for him and for everyone who knew him. It made him into a kind of monster.'

He paused and looked at her as if he expected her to comment on this. But Jade was still worrying about the Barmella thing and it took a moment to sink in.

'Your brother?' she said.

'That's right.'

So if he really is my father, Jade thought, then his brother would be my uncle. So now I have an uncle who's a kind of monster.

It got better and better.

'What kind of handicap?'

'It wasn't a physical handicap, as such. It wasn't something you could see. It was something in his mind.'

He was staring out of the window and following his gaze Jade saw little spirals of mist rising from the water and coiling around the seaplane like ghostly serpents.

'Have you ever heard of the Devil's Mirror?'

It struck a vague chord in Jade's memory but she shook her head.

'Well, the story goes that the Devil created a distorting mirror which made everything look bad and ugly. Even if it was good and beautiful. And he gave it to his demons and they took it all over the world until there was nowhere and no one that hadn't been distorted by it. Until finally the demons flew up to Heaven to show it to God and his angels to see what it would do to them – and on the way they dropped it.

'It fell to earth and smashed into a million pieces. And then it caused even more trouble because all the tiny splinters of glass went flying round the world and whenever a splinter flew into someone's eye it made that person see everything as bad and ugly.

Sometimes a splinter would get into someone's mind – and then it was even worse. And that is what happened to my brother.'

She must have looked a little doubtful about this because he gave her a sad little smile and said, 'I can see you don't believe me. Well, OK, it's just a story. The Devil's Mirror is a myth. But sometimes stories, or myths, are a way of telling the truth. Or of understanding a very complicated, very difficult subject.

'I did have a brother and he did have something inside him that made him see everything in a way that was distorted. Bad. Ugly. Frightening. Doctors gave it a name. They called it schizophrenia, from the Greek for "shattered mind". Shattered mind. Shattered mirror.'

'What happened to him?'

'I don't know. Our paths haven't crossed for a good many years. He caused a great deal of pain and unhappiness and suffering but . . .' he shrugged helplessly, 'it's because he sees everything through a piece of the Devil's Mirror. As bad and ugly. And so he wants to destroy them. And I think, deep down, he wants to destroy himself.'

Jade didn't know what to say. He suddenly seemed very sad and lonely.

'But just imagine if we could have seen this splinter, this tiny piece of glass, at the time of his birth, or even earlier – in the egg or the seed that he came from. And imagine we could take it out. Wouldn't that be wonderful?'

'But there *was* no splinter,' she protested. 'There *was* no Devil's Mirror.'

'Not as such. But there was something like it. Even if we call it by a different name. A code name.'

He leaned forward, gazing directly into her eyes, and she felt the extraordinary power of his conviction.

'Jade, everything we inherit from our parents – and I don't mean money or houses or things like that. I mean our looks, our colouring, whether we're fat or thin, stupid or clever, the talents we have and the problems, the diseases, mental and physical – all these things are written at the moment of conception, in the egg and in the seed that create us. They are written in something we call our genes – but they are written in code. We call it the genetic code.'

The code Aunt Em was working on . . .

'The problems my brother had were written in his genetic code. If we could have cracked that code and found the particular gene that gave him that problem and removed it . . .' he spread his arms again and the

180

dragon looked as if it was about to fly, 'all that suffering, all that pain, would never have happened. So I resolved that I would learn to crack the code – to find the bad genes and remove them, so that no one would ever suffer like my brother – and the people that suffered because of him.

'And so I became a geneticist. And I conducted experiments on human eggs that were not, I admit, permitted by English law. And for that they sent me to Houndwood.'

'But *why*?'

'Why?' He almost laughed. 'The big question. Why have certain people opposed every step in human progress since . . . well, almost since humans have existed? Why did the Church oppose the study of the human body? Why did they oppose the study of the stars and the planets? Why did they oppose the spread of knowledge? Why? I can't give you the answers to that, Jade, except that these things challenged their own powers, their prejudices, their own claims to have the answers to everything. And what the Church did then, the State does now but . . . here's a thing . . . Because they realized that what I was doing was so useful to society, so valuable, they built me a clinic and gave me a staff and allowed me to continue those experiments inside Houndwood. Because, whatever they say in public, and whatever the law says, they knew I was right. They know that some people are born with something in their genes that makes them dangerous. Dangerous to themselves and dangerous to society. So was I right to try to eliminate it – or was I wrong?'

He seemed to be waiting for Jade's opinion.

'But didn't you do something more than that?'

He sighed.

'I see that my friend Dr Mortlake has been getting at you. I did. And that is what I am going to tell you about because it affects you personally.'

Jade braced herself for more bad news.

'I have been talking about bad genes. But there are also good genes that are passed on by our parents. Genes that make people special – that give them special powers, talents, gifts, whatever you care to call them, and that enable them to become brilliant scientists or artists or athletes or . . . whatever. We call it the Genius Gene. And sometimes, in very rare cases, children inherit gifts and powers that we cannot explain. Powers that we describe as superhuman. The power to make objects move or change their shape in a way that defies the known

182

laws of physics, the power to heal or to look into the future, the power to read people's minds and bend them to their will.'

Despite the heat Jade suddenly felt cold.

How did he know?

Unless he really was her father . . . and the power came from him.

'Jade, I believe that these gifts, these energies, can be harnessed for the good of humankind. So . . . I found a number of donors. Seven to be exact. Seven women who had certain of these gifts or powers that I've mentioned. Not fully developed nor, in some cases, even recognized. They donated seven eggs for me to fertilize – and I screened them for faults: flaws, imperfections – to ensure they did not contain the condition that had afflicted my brother. Or any other problems that could be avoided.'

Dimly, in the back of her mind, she knew he was leaving something out – or she was missing something. But what?

'So now I had seven embryos – the fusing of egg and seed which can grow into a human child – and I planted those embryos in seven different women . . .'

'The surrogates.'

'Yes. The surrogates. She told you that?'

She nodded.

'And so you know that you are one of those children.'

He was watching her carefully. She nodded again. She did not trust herself to speak.

'Believe me, Jade, I fully intended to be there when you were born. I intended to be there while you were growing up. To be a real father to you. To guide you. To help you develop. And to develop those powers I hoped you would have. I wanted to be there for all of you but . . .' He raised his hands in that gesture of surrender or appeal. '. . . it was not to be. My plan was discovered. The children were taken from me. I was kept behind bars. And though I managed to escape I have been on the run ever since. But, Jade, believe me, I have never, ever given up the hope of getting you back. You and your brothers and sisters.'

'My brothers and sisters?' It was an astonishing concept to Jade. 'How many do I have?'

'Six. Three brothers, three sisters. I should say *half*-brothers and -sisters. Because you all had different mothers.'

'But where are they?'

'Ah. That is what I am hoping you will help me to find out.'

'Me?'

'Yes. You and your special gifts. Will you come with me and help me find them?'

19

Blackstakes Reach

The Goddess did indeed go like the Devil. And if it hadn't been for the lingering patches of mist and the rush-hour traffic and the professor's tendency to drift off on some endless monologue about the meaning of life or the origins of the Mafia and forget to keep his foot down they might have arrived by mid-morning. As it was they reached the sleepy village of Orford just as the church clock was striking twelve. It didn't seem to wake anyone up. The entire place seemed deserted.

But opposite the church was a pub.

The Furtive Fox.

Benedict left the professor in the car while he sought directions.

The sole occupant of the establishment was on the far side of the bar: a portly gentleman with a bald head and bushy ginger whiskers like a fox's tail stuck on his upper lip and flowing upwards across his cheeks. He was polishing beer glasses, doubtless in expectation of the lunchtime rush.

'The old flying boat base?' he frowned. 'You don't mean the old radar station?'

No, Benedict informed him patiently, he didn't mean the old radar station, unless it also catered for flying boats.

'Flying boats?' He shook his head as if the very idea was an abomination and eyed Benedict cautiously as if he might have escaped from somewhere – like Houndwood.

'Or seaplanes?'

It didn't help. But then the door opened and the rush arrived. A very old man and a very old dog.

'Morning, Trevor,' said mine host. 'Didn't happen to see a flying boat on the way in this morning, did you?' He gave him a wink and jerked his head in Benedict's direction as much as to say, we've got a right one here. 'Or a seaplane?'

'Heard about it, did you?' said the newcomer. 'And don't tell me I've been on the barley wine cos I ain't and it's still sitting there, large as life on Blackstakes Reach.'

'Eh?' The landlord gaped at him.

'Course use a drink now, though, after seeing that thing coming at me out of the mist. So while you're on your feet I'll have a pint of the usual.'

'Blackstakes Reach, you say?' ventured Benedict. 'And where exactly would that be?'

But this was a bit hasty for Orford, a bit presumptuous.

The old man waited until a foaming pint had been set in front of him, took a good long draught, set it down, wiped the creamy white line of froth from his upper lip and addressed himself to mine host as if Benedict wasn't there and had never spoken.

'Give me a right jolt when I seen it, I don't mind telling you. Out walking old Judy, I was, out on marsh. Looked up and there she were, coming in over reeds. Sets herself down on Blackstakes Reach neat as a whistle, over where the old flying boat station was. First I seen since the war. Thought I was back there for a minute.'

He turned and seemed to notice Benedict for the first time.

'Used to see 'em all the time in the war,' he

informed him loftily. 'Sunderlands and Catalinas, mostly. Big jobs. This weren't as big as they.' He turned back to the landlord. 'And bright yeller all over. Like a bloomin' great sunflower. I said to the old girl, we'll be seeing a Flying Fortress next. That's what Yanks used to fly in t'war,' he informed Benedict, in case he was having difficulty following the plot. 'And ole Jude chasing after her like a game 'un, weren't you, ole girl? Though she were a bloomin' great duck, I speck.'

Ole Jude gazed up at him gloomily.

'O' course she's not old enough to remember the flying boats, not by a long chalk . . .'

'Blackstakes Reach you say?' Benedict prompted him, thinking he could have gone fifteen rounds with the professor in the monologue stakes without breaking sweat. 'Can you get there by car?'

'You can,' said the old man. 'And then again you can't.'

He took another long pull of his pint.

'I see,' said Benedict, restraining a strong impulse to pour the rest of it over his head.

'Depending on whether you know the way.'

He finished his pint and caught Benedict's eye meaningfully.

Benedict laid a ten-pound note on the bar.

'Another glass of ale for the gentleman,' he said to the landlord, 'and one for yourself.'

'And a packet of salt and vinegar crisps,' said the old man.

Benedict waited until they were all happy and prepared to start again on the quest for directions but the old man took him by surprise. He swivelled on his heel like he was doing a robotic dance and pointed his stick at the door. The spaniel looked up in anticipation and cocked its ears.

'Straight through the village far as the river.'

He swivelled again, still pointing the stick and nearly taking Benedict's head off. 'Sharp left at the quay. Hundred yards and you come to a track. You'll see a sign saying No Motor Vehicles. Ignore it. Drive along the track for two miles and you'll come to the jetty on Blackstakes Reach. And there's she'll be. Bright yeller. Like a bloomin' great sunflower. Can't miss her. You a plane spotter then?'

But Benedict was on his way to the door.

The professor was not at all pleased about taking his precious Goddess along the muddy track. He drove at about two miles an hour and winced every time she went through a puddle.

'In your own time,' said Benedict. 'Don't feel you have to hurry.'

But the mist was much thicker down by the river and they could barely see the reed beds at the water's edge. On the other side of the track there was nothing: no trees, no bushes, just the marsh grass wet with fog and once a concrete bunker, left over from the war. Then they saw a sign that read: Ministry of Defence. Danger Area. Unexploded Bombs. No Admittance.

The professor stopped the car.

'That's it,' he said firmly. 'I'm not going a yard further.'

'It's an old sign,' Benedict attempted to persuade him. 'From the last war.'

'It is certainly not an old sign. It's newly painted.'

This appeared to be true.

Benedict sighed.

'All right,' he said. 'I'll go on by myself.'

He started to open the door but then the mist lifted a little and he saw it. A bright-yellow seaplane. Exactly where the old man said it would be, at the end of a long jetty.

But on the opposite side of the river.

'Well,' said the professor grumpily. 'The old girl's got us this far but she can't drive across water.'

Benedict was looking at the map. There was a bridge about five miles ahead but it was a footbridge and there was no road marked on the far side of the river, not even a track. It seemed to be a long bank of shingle between the river and the North Sea.

'Well, I suppose I could swim over,' he said without enthusiasm.

'Or we could take a boat,' said the professor.

It wasn't an entirely frivolous remark. He pointed through the window to the edge of the water where, part hidden among the reeds, was a long, low skiff, the kind used for hunting duck.

And then he asked the question that had been vaguely on his mind ever since they had left Oxford.

'But what are we going to do when we get there?'

20

Jade's Choice

'Your carriage awaits,' said Dr Kobal. He indicated the yellow seaplane at the end of the jetty.

Jade stared at it.

'You want me to go in *that*?'

'What do you mean "*that*"?' He sounded indignant. 'It's the very latest model – and I've only crashed it twice.'

Then suddenly he was serious.

'Jade – we haven't got a lot of time. Other people are interested in this special talent of yours. That's why I had to act now.'

'What other people?'

The men in the masks? The people at Houndwood?

'I'll tell you when we're on our way.'

He was gazing at her with an intensity she found uncomfortable but also . . . tempting. Challenging. As if everything was possible and there was a whole world of adventure waiting on a single word.

Like this exotic rainforest filled with tropical birdsong – in the middle of a drab English estuary – in November.

She shook her head. This was madness. And yet . . .

Hadn't she wanted something interesting to happen?

Yes, but not *that* interesting . . .

She had a sudden memory of when she was little and her father – or at least the man she had believed was her father – reading bedtime stories to her. Whenever he got bored and wanted her to go to sleep he'd make up a different ending. Like in *Cinderella* when he reached the part where the fairy godmother said, 'You *shall* go to the ball' and he'd make Cinderella say: 'But I have to do the ironing.'

And then he'd turn to the last page and read: 'And so the fairy godmother turned into a pumpkin and Cinderella got on with the ironing. The end.'

And half laughing, half indignant Jade would shout: 'No, she didn't. No, it isn't.'

And her father would say, 'I bet that's what would happen in real life.'

The memory brought a lump to her throat.

'I mean,' said Dr Kobal with a grin, 'do you have anything better to do?'

Only an essay on woodland food chains for Miss Simpson.

She looked out of the window at the yellow seaplane with its congregation of ducks.

She looked back at Dr Kobal in his gorgeous kimono.

Her father.

Impossible.

But why else was he doing this? Why was she so important to him?

'You know,' he said, 'don't you? You know this is what you have to do. You have to bring us all together. As a family. Your *real* family.'

For a moment, for one mad moment, she almost said yes.

But it wouldn't be right. She couldn't leave her parents. Not like that. Even if they weren't her real parents. Even if they'd lied to her. They'd looked after her all her life and they loved her. Didn't they? And they'd be out of their minds with worry . . .

She shook her head. 'I'll have to talk to my . . . my parents,' she said.

'Ah, well I'm afraid that might be a bit difficult,' said Dr Kobal. 'They'd call the police, you see, and I'd be locked up again.'

'But if I talked it over with them,' she insisted desperately. 'I could come and see you . . .'

'Do you really think so?'

But no, she didn't really think so.

'Well, it's your choice,' he said. 'I can't force you to come with me. That is, I *won't* force you. You have to make the decision yourself. Of your own free will. It's one of the conditions.'

A voice from the foot of the stairs.

'The pilot wish to speak with you.'

They looked down. The nurse – Barmella.

'He says we have a problem.'

Dr Kobal stood up.

'I'll leave you to think it over,' he said to Jade.

'I have the juice,' said Barmella.

She was carrying a tray with a glass of orange juice on it and a plate of chocolate biscuits.

Kobal frowned. He looked at Jade again as if he was thinking something over. Then he said: 'Very well. Carry on.'

And with a swish of his golden gown he was gone.

Jade sat alone at the table staring out over the water. The mist seemed to be getting worse. She could only just make out the plane at the end of the jetty.

If she didn't go with them he'd go away and she'd never see him again, or her mysterious brothers and sisters. She'd go back to Turnham Green and life would carry on the same as before. Or she'd be locked up in 'the Annex' at Houndwood while they did experiments on her, like an animal in a cage. A guinea pig.

A pair of white swans came gliding out of the mist and the ducks moved back to a respectful distance. As the swans looked up at the great yellow bird that had invaded their territory, one of them raised itself part out of the water and flapped its wings as if it was trying to scare it away.

And the ugly duckling went back to the farmyard and the other ducks pecked it to bits. The end.

Jade drank the orange juice that Barmella had set down in front of her.

She couldn't deal with this. It was all too much – and it was all happening far too fast.

The mist seemed to be even thicker, and darker.

She could barely see out of the windows. And then she realized it wasn't the mist. It was her eyes. They were losing focus. And her head felt so heavy. All she wanted to do was sleep.

She didn't wake up, even when the glass smashed on the floor and her head crashed down on the table.

21

Messing About on the River

The mist had grown much worse.

It was impossible to see either bank of the river, let alone the aircraft at the end of the jetty.

'We'll cut her moorings,' Benedict had explained to the professor, 'and let her drift with the current.'

But the current was proving more of a problem for them at the moment. The punt had no pole and they were forced to paddle with their bare hands. It was tiring work and Benedict suspected they were drifting downriver. Besides, he was much stronger than the professor and even though he was using his left arm and the professor his right he wondered if they were just going round in circles.

'It's no good,' the professor gasped. 'I'm going to have to stop for a bit.'

He took his hand out of the water and flexed the fingers, his face screwed up in agony. The water was bitingly cold. Benedict peered through swirling mist and thought he caught a glimpse of reeds at the water's edge.

'One more effort,' he said. 'We're nearly there.'

But was it the far bank or the one they had started from?

He stretched out full length in the bows and paddled furiously with both arms. Moments later they were in among the reeds. An indignant pair of water hens shot out with loud cries and went scooting off into the mist.

The professor laughed almost hysterically. He looked exhausted.

A sudden wind rustled through the reeds. Then they heard another noise – like a speedboat bearing down on them. And something else – a kind of thumping in the air. And then out of the mist, flying low over the water, came two white swans, beating the air with their wings as they strove for height.

And behind them, throwing up two great plumes of water, the seaplane.

It rose above the swans, missing them by the length of a tail feather, and vanished into the mist.

The two men clung to the sides of the lurching punt.

'That,' said the professor, 'was quite a sight.'

'But not quite what we wanted to see,' Benedict pointed out.

'So what now?'

'Back to the car,' said Benedict.

The professor collapsed theatrically in the bottom of the boat.

'Come on,' said Benedict. 'You know how much you enjoy messing about on the river. You can be Mole and I'll be Ratty.'

He found a piece of driftwood among the reeds and used it as an oar but it still took them the best part of an hour to paddle the punt back to the far shore and find the Citroën in the mist.

The professor switched the engine on and they gradually thawed out in the blast from the heater. For a while all they could think about was the pain of returning circulation.

Then the professor said: 'They must be mad trying to take off in that. A thick fog and no guide lights. If they'd hit either of those swans they'd be dead in the water.'

'Maybe they saw us coming,' Benedict proposed. He clenched and unclenched his fists to get the blood flowing.

'Any idea where they might be heading?'

'If it's who I think it is, a lake on the Finnish–Russian border – about two hundred miles north of the Arctic Circle.'

The professor looked incredulous.

'Well, they won't get there today,' he said.

Benedict looked at his watch. It was a few minutes after two.

'I don't see why not. It's about a three-hour flight to Helsinki – maybe a couple more to the Russian border.'

'In a jetliner, maybe. Not in that thing.'

'So how long . . . ?'

'I read up the stats on the Heron. Fully loaded, she's got a maximum range of about six hundred miles. It must be about fifteen hundred to the Russian border.'

'So . . . ?'

'They'll have to come down for fuel. Twice. And they won't want to take off and land in the dark. Not on water. So that means an overnight.'

The light was already fading from the sky. They

could see the beacon from the lighthouse at Orford Ness beaming out over the North Sea.

'So how far d'you reckon they'll get before dark?'

The professor shrugged. 'Denmark? Norway at a pinch. My guess is they'll put her down on a fjord. Air Traffic Control could track them on radar. They could have the police waiting for them when they come down. If you're sure they've got the girl with them.'

Benedict shook his head. 'I don't want the police involved,' he said. 'Not yet.'

He saw the look on the professor's face.

'I told you it was deep,' he said.

'I think you'd better tell me a bit more than that. This is a young girl we're talking about. We've got her safety to consider.'

Benedict did not answer for a moment. Then he said: 'I know this man. If we bring the police into it we'll never see her again. But if I could somehow get there before them . . . I think I'd be able to get her away from him before any harm comes to her.'

'You think?'

'I know.'

'And what's your interest in this? I'm sorry to have to ask you but . . .'

'It's a Church matter. I can't tell you more than that. But I will tell you this. If we involve the police she could be in very great danger. More than she's in already.'

The professor rubbed a hand across his jaw. 'So where do we go from here?'

'How fast does that thing go – as you seem to know so much about it.'

'At an altitude of ten thousand feet she has a cruising speed of a hundred and twenty knots – that's about a hundred and fifty miles an hour to you.'

'So if you're right they won't arrive at their eventual destination until about this time tomorrow.'

'Not unless they put the wheels down and land at a regular airport to take on fuel – and they can't very well do that with the child aboard.'

'So in theory I could get there before them.'

'If you had access to a private jet and we could get to an airport in time.'

'You wouldn't happen to . . .'

The professor sighed and slipped the car into gear.

'I knew you were going to ask that,' he said.

22

The Arctic Patrol

'Well, what do you think?' enquired the professor as they gazed out across the runway.

A large military aircraft stood in a pool of portable floodlights; surrounding it – like piglets nuzzling at a fat sow – a small fleet of service vehicles.

It wasn't private and it wasn't a jet but it would get Benedict to the far north of Lapland in a little under eight hours, the professor assured him, and it wouldn't cost him a penny.

'What is it?' demanded Benedict suspiciously, 'and how did you get it?'

'Well, it's only borrowed, dear boy, only borrowed,' said the professor.

The fog had lifted and it had taken them less than

an hour to drive to the air base, with Benedict at the wheel and the professor on the phone: 'calling in a favour' – as he put it – from someone at the US Embassy in London.

The result was sitting on the runway.

She was an Orion maritime patrol aircraft, the professor explained in that lofty tone he adopted when displaying his knowledge of cars, planes and other grown-up toys – used mainly for anti-submarine warfare and reconnaisance.

But he was less forthcoming about how he had managed to persuade the US Navy to carry a civilian passenger on a flight to Lapland.

'I told them you were an emissary from the Pope sent on a diplomatic mission to Santa Claus,' he told Benedict, 'and that the whole future of Christmas might depend on it.'

Benedict assumed he was joking – though with the professor you could never be sure.

The skipper of the plane clearly thought Benedict was some kind of spook on a mission for the intelligence services.

'The nearest NATO base to Russia – at least the nearest we can land you – is at Porsanger,' he explained in the briefing room, indicating a point on the map at the extreme northern tip of Norway. 'But you'll have to make your own way from there.'

The distance from Porsanger to Lake Piru looked to be no more than about one hundred miles but Benedict had no idea what the roads were like or even if they were open at this time of the year. He put a call through to Jussa Proksi on his mobile and the shaman promised to have a vehicle waiting for him at the airport. He didn't say whether it would be a car or a reindeer sled.

'I'm sorry I can't come with you,' the professor said. 'But I have a tutorial tomorrow on Modern Vampirism. Do let me know how you get on.'

They took off at 1600 hours and headed out over the North Sea. The sun was a veiled orange orb in the sky behind them, the world ahead curving into darkness. They would stay well out from land as far north as Bergen, the navigator told Benedict, and then hug the Norwegian coast for a thousand miles north to Porsanger. Benedict had the impression they made the trip fairly regularly – they called it the Arctic patrol – but he didn't ask too many questions.

The plane had a crew of ten, most of whom were situated in a cramped space behind the flight deck, which they called the Ops Room, with enough computers to fight their own global conflict. The flight engineer reeled them off proudly like a car salesman showing off the latest model: acoustic sensor suite, infrared detection system, magnetic anomaly detectors, sonar, radar . . . The professor would have loved it. Benedict tried to look like he was taking it all in. They found him a seat next to one of the big round windows that bulged out from the hull. Not that they called it a window. They called it a 180-degree surveillance site.

'Make yourself comfortable,' the navigator told him. 'You've got nothing to do but eat and sleep for the next eight hours – or you can watch a DVD if you like. We got a great library of horror movies.'

Benedict was quite content to look out of the 180-degree surveillance site. Above the cloud cover there was a magnificent view of the galaxy and he occupied himself with picking out the main constellations It was the first time he hadn't felt nervous flying. The plane was so crammed with electronics it didn't seem possible for anything to go wrong – unless someone put a horror movie into the magnetic anomaly detector by mistake. He was so relaxed he fell asleep.

He slept for about four hours and it would have

been longer if one of the crew members hadn't woken him up.

'We've got some weather,' he said. 'Better fasten your seat belt.'

Benedict just had time to notice that the stars had disappeared. The next moment the plane dropped like a stone, leaving his stomach glued to the cabin roof, and he heard the four engines screaming as they clawed at the thin Arctic air.

23

How Life Began, Why It Went All Pear-Shaped and What Keeps Planes in the Air

The professor was right about the Heron. She could only fly for about four hours without coming down for fuel. But he was wrong about *where* she would come down.

Three and a half hours after taking off from Orford Ness, she lowered her wheels and landed like any normal aircraft at a commercial airport.

Stavanger Airport, in Norway.

So there was no problem landing and taking off in the dark. And because she was in transit — and officially bound for Russia – they were not troubled by officials from customs or immigration. No one suspected there was a kidnapped child sleeping in the dimly lit cabin.

An hour later, with her fuel tanks filled, the Snipe took off again, heading north-east towards Sweden.

Jade slept on. She did not wake up until they were taking off from their next stop – Lulea Airport on the Gulf of Bothnia. Not that she knew this. For the first minute or two she didn't even know which planet she was on.

She had slept through the near death experience with the swans at Orford Ness; through the long flight over the North Sea as the world spun into darkness; and through the stopovers in Norway and Sweden. Her mind was a blank page waiting for memory to come and write something on it.

She turned her head – and sitting next to her was the nurse. Barmella. With cans on, listening to music on an iPod.

Then memory came flooding back and she tried to stand up.

But she was strapped into her seat and her legs felt weak.

Barmella took the cans off and put her hand on Jade's forehead.

Angrily Jade shook it off.

'Where am I?' she demanded. 'Where are you taking me?'

'You are in airplane,' said Barmella. 'Stay in seat.'

Jade peered out of the window in alarm. She could see a light flashing on and off, illuminating a small patch of wing. Otherwise nothing. No stars, no moon, no lights on the ground below.

'Why? Where are we flying to?' she cried out, but Barmella had disappeared through a door at the front of the tiny cabin.

Her mouth felt very dry and her head was fuzzy.

She remembered the glass of orange juice in the conservatory.

They must have drugged her.

The door opened again and Dr Kobal appeared.

He was no longer wearing a golden kimono but the effect was almost as dazzling. He was dressed all in white. White shirt hanging over baggy white pants, white trainers. White socks, too, in all probability. And a big grin on his face.

'Jade,' he said.

She turned her head away and looked out of the window.

He sat down next to her.

'I know you won't believe me,' he said, 'but I am really very, very sorry about this.'

'Then take me back home.'

He sighed.

'I can't do that. Not right now.'

She looked at him.

'Where are you taking me?'

'Lapland,' he said casually. 'We've just entered Finnish air space as a matter of fact. We should be arriving in an hour or so.'

Lapland? Finnish air space?

She stared out of the window in panic.

'But . . . *why*?' It came out as a kind of wail.

'I told you – we're going to find your brothers and sisters. We're going to be a family.'

'But you said it was my choice. You said—'

'I know, I know,' he said soothingly. 'And I meant it – at the time. But my hand was forced. And be honest, isn't it what you wanted? Deep down? Aren't you relieved you didn't have to make the choice for yourself?'

'That's not true. And it's not the point. It was my

own free will; that's what you said. You said you wouldn't force me.'

'I know, I know, and I'm very sorry it had to happen the way it did. But I couldn't do anything about it. There was someone out there who was trying to kill you.'

'Kill me?' She stared at him. '*Why?*'

'Because of what you are.'

Jade put her hand up to her forehead. She could feel a migraine coming on.

Because of what I am.

'*Who* was trying to kill me?' she demanded. 'I don't believe you.'

'Well, I can't say I blame you and it's difficult to explain right now but let's just say someone who thinks you should never have been born.'

Jade felt a strange feeling in the pit of her stomach, a hollow feeling like when you've had nothing to eat. But it wasn't because she was hungry.

'Why? Because I'm a freak, some kind of *monster*?' Jade was close to tears now. 'And why *was* I born? Mixed up in a . . . in a *dish*.' She remembered the broken egg in the Petri dish . . . 'And planted in some . . . in some *mother hen*. Why? What was the point?'

'Well, it wasn't a hen, actually. That's not how it works but . . .'

But then he caught her eye and decided this wasn't the right approach.

'What was the point?' He put his head back and gazed at the ceiling, as if he was trying to remember.

Then he glanced sideways at her, his eyes teasing.

'Is there any point in saying because I wanted a little girl just like you?'

'No,' she said angrily, brushing the tears from her eyes, 'none at all.'

Barmella came back with a glass of what looked like water.

'And you can take that away,' Jade said. 'I'm not being drugged again.'

Kobal took it and drank a mouthful and then passed it to Jade.

'No drugs,' he said. 'Just ordinary iced water. Drink. I'm sure you're feeling thirsty.'

Jade took the glass and turned it away so she wouldn't be drinking from the same side as him.

'OK,' he said. 'Why were you born? Why was *I* born? Why is anyone born?'

She waited for him to tell her. He seemed to have all the answers.

'No, come on,' he said. 'Why do people have babies?'

'Because they love them,' she said sulkily.

'How can they love them? They haven't been born.'

'All right. Because they love each other. And they want to make a baby together. That's what *should* happen. Not . . . not the way it happened with me.'

'OK. OK. That's a good answer. And in a perfect world it would be enough. But it's not, is it? It's far from perfect. It's a mess.'

'But that's nothing to do with people loving each other,' Jade almost shouted at him. 'It's nothing to do with people having babies.'

'No? Let me tell you a story.'

'Is it another story like the Devil's Mirror?' She meant it to be scathing.

'A bit like the Devil's Mirror,' he admitted with a shrug, 'but you've probably heard this one. One of the versions anyway. It's the story of Creation. God creates the world and the heavens and all that is in them and the very last thing he creates is Man. And he calls him Adam.'

'Why?'

'What do you mean, why?'

'Why does he call him Adam?'

'I don't know.' For the first time he sounded irritated. 'Nobody's ever asked me that before. I expect it was the first name that occurred to him. And because Adam was lonely he created Woman. Eve. And they lived in the Garden of Eden and then what?'

'Don't you know?'

'Yes, of course I know – I want *you* to tell me.'

'God tells them they can do whatever they like as long as they don't eat from the Tree of Knowledge and then the Serpent comes and persuades Eve to eat an apple and she persuades Adam to eat some of it and God kicks them out of the Garden and they die. The end.'

He stared at her for a moment as if she was starting to get under his skin but then he thought about it and shrugged again.

'Well, I suppose that just about sums it up. Though it was a pear, not an apple – not many people know that – and it would be better to say, To be Continued, not The End. And you've missed something – something very important. The motivation for the whole plot. Why did the Serpent do it?'

'You're asking me?'

'I'm asking you.'

'How would I know?'

'Well, who *was* the Serpent?'

'Satan.'

'Right, Satan – and where did Satan come from?'

'Hell.'

'Before that. Before he was in Hell.'

'Search me.'

Jade hadn't been brought up to be religious. All she knew about the Bible was a few stories her teachers had told them in school. She had no idea where Satan was supposed to have come from.

'OK,' said Dr Kobal, who was sounding more and more like her teachers. 'In the story – the Creation story – before ever there were human beings on the world – or animals or plants or anything else – or even before there was a world – what were there?'

Jade thought about it.

'Stars?'

'Stars. Interesting.' He seemed to drift off into a world of his own. 'I was thinking of angels – but angels and stars . . . well . . .'

'Angels?' Jade repeated drily, as if he had said fairies. But at the same time she felt a kind of shiver run through her. She'd always had a bit of a thing about angels, even if they *were* a myth.

'Yes. Angels. And quite a few of these angels were not at all happy when God decided to create humans. Their argument was, why create a race of inferior beings, a species of ape, when you've got us? It seemed to them to be an extremely weird thing to do. The whim of a foolish old man in his dotage. To create this beautiful world and then create these monster apes and make them the masters of it and tell the angels they've got to be their servants. It seemed to them that this was sheer madness – and that sooner or later the apes were going to run riot and smash and kill and destroy everything in sight. And when God wouldn't listen to them they rebelled. And they elected Satan as their leader. Except that he wasn't called Satan then – that was a name that came much later on – he was called Lucifer, or the Shining One. Well, the rebellion failed and the rebel angels were cast into outer darkness, or Hell, and became known as demons and the humans went on to do exactly what they'd said they'd do which was to make one almighty cock-up of everything.'

'Didn't the demons have something to do with that?'

'What do you mean?'

'Well, as I recall,' said Jade, with icy politeness, 'didn't the demons tempt them into doing all the things they were told not to do?'

'Well, if they did, doesn't that just go to show they were right – and that humans couldn't be trusted.'

Jade shrugged again. 'Well, in any case, it's just a story,' she said. 'A myth.'

'And what did I tell you about myths?'

'They're a way of telling the truth. Or explaining difficult subjects. Not that you'd know anything about the truth,' she added witheringly.

'OK. Let's look at the other explanation. The scientific explanation. That there was no God. No Creation. That the world evolved over millions of years. And everything in it, including apes. But how did the apes evolve into humans?'

'Dunno,' said Jade, just to provoke him.

'Of course you know. Think.'

Jade thought about what she had been told about the theory of evolution and a phrase came to mind.

'Survival of the fittest?'

'Survival of the fittest. Exactly. Except that in this case the fittest were the cleverest. The ones that "ate from the tree of knowledge". The ones clever enough to adapt to their environment – to make it work *for* them instead of against them. And so they became the masters of the planet. But because deep down they were all still apes – and not half as clever as they thought they were – they began to destroy the environment. Just like the rebel angels said they would in the story – the myth. And unless someone does something about it, they will destroy the planet – and everything in it, including themselves. Unless – what?'

'Unless they change.'

'At last. An intelligent answer. *Unless they change.* And for the first time we have the ability to change. To make a different kind of human. To modify the species. Just as we have modified plants and animals.

'That is why I brought you into the world – you and your brothers and sisters. You are the first. The prototypes. If all goes according to plan many more will follow you.'

There was far too much to think about here. Jade could feel a migraine coming on.

'And what makes you think we'll be any better than the last lot?' she said.

'Because you will be more like angels than apes.'

She regarded him thoughtfully.

'Do you believe in angels?' For a moment she had forgotten to be angry with him.

'Of course I do,' he said. 'Don't you?'

'I'd like to,' she admitted, 'but . . . why is it we never see them?'

'Because you're not meant to. The angels are the watchers. They see you but you never see them. Besides,' he looked at her with a curious smile, 'how would you know if you did? Do you think they have wings, like in the pictures?'

'So – do you believe in all the rest of it – in God and the Devil and that?'

'What do you mean, do I believe in them? Do I believe in everything they tell me?'

'No. Do you believe they exist?'

'Of course they exist. I've met them several times. Charming people, both of them. Never could understand why they couldn't get on.'

What was the use? She was about to make some cutting remark when she became aware of the looming presence of Barmella.

'The pilot wish to speak with you,' she said.

Kobal made his way forward and Barmella took one of the facing seats opposite. Jade studied her face for scar tissue. She had the weird notion that she was

222

the doll come back to haunt her. Of course, it couldn't be true but it was no weirder than some of the things that had been happening to her lately.

Kobal returned from speaking to the pilot.

'We've got a bit of a problem,' he said.

'Someone else trying to kill me?' said Jade, meaning it to be sarcastic but bracing herself all the same.

'Not someone as such. The weather.'

Jade looked out of the window but all she could see was the light flashing on the wing.

'There's a storm coming in from the Arctic. Vromski thought we could outrun it but we can't.'

Jade spoke casually but Jade sensed this was serious.

'So what can we do?' she said.

'Well, we can't go over it and we can't go round it, so we're just going to have to go through it.'

'Can we do that?' asked Barmella.

'Probably,' he said.

Then he went away again.

Moments later the storm hit them. Or they hit the storm. Jade wasn't sure how it worked if you were in a plane flying at over a hundred miles an hour. All she knew was that they were thrown about like a . . . well, like a leaf in a storm. She still couldn't see anything out of the window but she had the impression that the overall direction was downward.

Then Dr Kobal came back and sat down again. Or, it would be more accurate to say, was hurled into the seat next to her.

'Problem,' he said.

'What now?' said Barmella.

'Vromski says there's ice forming on the wings.'

'What does that mean?' Jade demanded anxiously.

'Well, how do you think planes fly?' he asked her.

'I don't know.' It seemed a bit late for a lesson on the subject.

'Well, the way the wings are shaped they direct more air under them than over them,' Dr Kobal explained calmly. 'So the air under the wings lifts the plane up and keeps it flying. When the pilot wants to come down he changes the shape of the wings with something we call flaps so there's more air on top than there is underneath and this brings us down – gradually. But if ice forms on the wings it changes the equation.'

'But what does it *mean*?' Jade almost wailed.

'It means we're going to crash,' said Dr Kobal.

24

Off the Radar

Brother Benedict stepped out of the overheated cabin of the Orion and into the biting cold of an Arctic winter. But he was very glad to be on solid ground again, even if it was covered with snow and the temperature ten degrees below zero.

The Orion had risen majestically above the storm but it had still been a rough ride at times and his fear of flying was as strong as it had ever been.

The skipper saw him off the ship – as he called it – and shook his hand and solemnly wished him luck. It was obvious he thought he was a spy heading for Russia, though there must have been easier ways of getting there, Benedict reflected. And Russia was no longer the favourite place for spies. There were new enemies now.

There was a thin snow falling and the wind felt like sandpaper on his cheeks.

He was relieved to find Jussa Proksi waiting for him in the terminal building but the shaman had news for him.

'They come down,' he said.

Benedict was confused. Did he mean they'd got to Lake Piru before him? But no, he didn't mean that. He meant they were down in the forest.

'I have contact in Air Control who keep track of them,' he said. 'He call me before you land and say they vanish off radar forty minutes after they cross into Finland.'

'Did they put out a distress call?'

'No. Nothing. But there is bad weather in the area. He say they come down. Crash. Ka-boom. They make alarm. Send out search and rescue.'

Jussa had brought a pick-up truck with a snowplough attached to the front. They sat in the cab and consulted the map.

'The plane go off radar here.' Jussa indicated a point about a hundred miles into Finland and about the same distance from Lake Piru.

The map was full of lakes.

'Could they have put down on one?' Benedict ventured.

'Maybe,' Jussa conceded. 'But the lakes now freeze with ice — with snow on top, very thick. We have twenty-centimetre fall in last day. Is not easy to land on frozen lake at night.'

'Even so.' Benedict scrutinized the map. 'If they survived the crash, they will be trying to get to the castle. If you were them, what route would you take?'

'On ground?' Jussa thought about it. 'Well, is not many. And they not have vehicle, I think.'

'They could have skis,' Benedict suggested. 'Even a snowmobile.'

The shaman regarded him curiously.

'This man, then, he not wait for search and rescue?'

'Not if he can avoid it. He's rather keen not to be found by the authorities.'

'Well, there is trail, here.' Jussa drew his finger across the map in a line from west to east. 'Ski trail through forest. From Swedish border almost to Lake Piru. Is use for *langlauf* — cross-country skiing. Also, by herders for round up reindeer. But is cover with snow, very thick, this time of year.'

Benedict looked carefully at the route. A wild guess grew to a conviction.

'That is the route he will take,' he said.

He saw that it crossed two roads – the only roads running from the south to the far north. He pointed to one of the crossing points.

'Can we drive there?'

'Of course.' Jussa shrugged. 'In this we drive anywhere.'

He put the truck into gear.

'And can you get us any back-up?'

'You think we need?'

'I think it would be wise.'

The shaman fished out his mobile phone.

'And I think you wish they bring guns,' he said, 'as you are a man of religion.'

25

Down in the Forest

Jade was drawn up in the crash position, as described in her survivors' handbook. Hands on head, head bent forward over her knees, feet planted firmly on the floor and as far back as they would go.

She was very, very scared. As scared as anyone can be who thinks they are going to die in a plane crash. But after a while, when they still hadn't crashed, she felt more uncomfortable than frightened. She was so scrunched up she could hardly breathe. She began to hope they might not crash at all and that Dr Kobal would come back and say, 'False alarm', in that laconic way of his, and they could get on with discussing the meaning of life and where babies and serpents came from.

She sat up straight for a moment to catch her breath and snatched a quick look through the window, but all she could see were shreds of cloud rushing past and droplets of water streaking across the glass. Then Barmella pushed her down again. The noise from the engines was terrible and just went on and on – a kind of racing-to-destruction noise, and the whole plane was vibrating and lurching from side to side.

Then they crashed.

At first it just felt like a very bad landing. Like when the pilot comes down too fast and you bounce, hitting the runway. But then they hit it again and this time Jade felt the shock through the whole airframe and the lights went out and the overhead lockers flew open and things fell out of them and there was a smell of smoke or burning rubber and a horrible grinding, screaming noise like metal on metal. She risked another quick look out of the window and glimpsed trees rushing past the wing tip and then Barmella shoved her head back down again and she closed her eyes and prayed.

And amazingly it worked; or something did. Because they were slowing down and she felt them sliding to one side. Then there was a terrible jolt and the seat belt practically cut her in half and they were skewing right round as if they were in a whirligig at a funfair and then there was an enormous bang, lots of smoke . . . and then silence.

She opened her eyes. There was a Christmas tree sticking through the side of the cabin. Snow was billowing in through the hole it had made. She looked at Barmella. She was still doubled up in the crash position . . . And then she saw the blood oozing out from under her hair.

She knew you had to get out fast – but how? And what about everyone else? She slipped the catch on her seat belt and climbed over Barmella and made her way forward, ducking under the branches of the fir tree.

The door to the flight deck was hanging open and she peered in through the smoke . . .

Into a scene from a nightmare . . .

It was a charnel house. A tree – a much larger tree than the one in the cabin – had smashed in through the front of the cockpit and two bodies, presumably the pilot and the co-pilot, were impaled on its branches. Kobal, her father, sat just behind them, still strapped into his seat but with a gaping wound in his neck that almost separated his head from his body.

She only knew it was him from the clothes he wore, that had once been so white . . .

She reeled back into the cabin and was violently sick.

Then she heard a groan.

Barmella.

She crawled back under the tree and freed her from the seat belt. But she was still only half-conscious, and when Jade tried to drag her out of her seat she sprawled into the aisle and lay there unmoving. The cabin was now almost filled with smoke – and there was a terrible smell of aviation fuel.

She wondered if she could crawl through the hole the tree had made but it was almost blocked with branches; even if she could squeeze through herself she'd never get Barmella through. Then she remembered the emergency exit at the rear of the cabin.

She dragged the nurse along the floor towards it. There was a light above the door and a handle that said Pull in Emergencies Only.

Jade pulled . . .

And then the door wasn't there any more. Just a gaping great hole and a blast of freezing-cold air and the swirling snow.

A bright-yellow escape chute had dropped down at her feet and she managed to heave Barmella up so she was sitting in the open doorway. Then she gave her a shove and watched as she slid down and landed in a heap at the bottom. Like a broken doll.

She looked back down the smoke-filled cabin, thinking she should try and find some blankets, warm clothing, anything to stop them freezing to death . . . but then she caught a flicker of flame from the flight deck beyond the fallen tree. It could go up at any second . . .

She took a deep breath and leaped into space, landing on Barmella with both feet . . .

The nurse groaned and staggered up, looking around in total incomprehension.

'What happen?' she began. 'Where is Dr Kobal?'

'Dead,' said Jade. 'And we will be too if we don't get away from here.'

She dragged at her arm and together they staggered away into the snow.

She didn't stop until they were about a hundred metres away from the crashed plane. Then she looked back, and for the first time she had a clear picture of what had happened.

They had landed on a frozen lake covered in deep

snow. She could see the long swathe the plane had cut into it before ploughing into the trees. The nose was all crumpled up as far as the cockpit and one wing was sticking up at a strange angle. She looked like a great yellow bird with a broken wing.

Jade could still smell the aviation fuel . . . but there was no fire.

She must have imagined the flames on the flight deck – or else the snow had put them out. The trees must have dumped half a ton on her when she hit them.

But now it wasn't fire she feared; it was the cold.

Until now she had been fortified by adrenalin . . . and distracted by fear. Now for the first time she realized how incredibly cold it was. A vicious wind hurled snow and chips of ice across the frozen lake and howled through the trees like a pack of wolves. She was shivering uncontrollably and Barmella was like a frozen corpse already.

They had to find shelter. But where?

Then she knew.

'We've got to get back to the plane,' she shouted through chattering teeth.

Barmella nodded and staggered to her feet, and together they stumbled back through the snow towards the stricken plane.

They were almost there when a figure appeared in the open doorway.

The shock drove all other thoughts from Jade's mind – all fears of cold and fire. She even stopped shivering and a strange, unearthly wail gathered deep in her throat and leaked out through her gaping mouth . . .

Because it was Kobal.

His white shirt and pants were drenched in blood and he looked like a ghoul from the deepest depths of Hell but there was no sign of that terrible wound in his neck and he was holding a fire extinguisher in his hand.

'What you guys doing out there?' he said in a tone of mild surprise. 'Come back in before you catch your death of cold.'

26

Ambushed . . .

Kobal leaned out to haul Jade back up into the wreck. She snatched a quick look at his neck but all she could see was a livid red mark, like a rash or a nervous flush. If there *had* been a wound it had mysteriously healed. Unless she had imagined it.

But where had all the blood come from?

'Vromski's dead,' he told Barmella, 'and the co-pilot. He did well to get us down on the lake but he couldn't stop her sliding on the ice.'

He found a first-aid box in one of the lockers and dressed the cut on her forehead while Jade wrapped herself up in a blanket and huddled in one of the seats. She was still shivering, but despite the damage the plane sheltered them from the worst of the snow and the wind and there no longer seemed to be any danger of fire. They could sit it out here until they were rescued, she thought.

But Kobal's next words made her think again.

'Get these on,' he said, throwing her a bundle of clothing, 'and we'll be on our way.'

On our way?

What was he going to do, take off with no wheels and a smashed wing? Somehow she wouldn't have been surprised.

But no. Apparently he had other plans.

They had all the survival kit they needed, he said, and it was only eighty miles to the castle.

'We're going to walk there?' Jade stared at him as if he was insane.

'Only part of the way,' he said. 'Then we'll get some help.'

What help?

But he was pulling boots from a locker and some strange objects that looked like old-fashioned tennis racquets.

Snowshoes.

She'd seen them in films of the Inuit but she'd never thought anyone would expect her to wear them.

'What am I supposed to do with these?' She gazed

at them in bewilderment, turning them over in her hands.

'You put one foot in front of the other,' he said cuttingly, 'and then do the same with the second foot. It's called walking. Much better than crawling once you get used to it, especially in snow.'

She continued to protest, but he was busy packing supplies into a backpack and she realized she was wasting her breath. The bundle of clothing turned out to be a ski suit and there were several pairs of boots to choose from. She found a pair that just about fitted her.

Barmella seemed to have recovered from her knock on the head. She threw the snowshoes out into the snow, handed Jade a pair of goggles and invited her to slide down the chute after them.

What would they do if she refused?

She didn't care to put it to the test. She pulled up the hood of the ski suit, fitted the goggles on, and slid down the chute.

Kobal was trying to make a call on his mobile – to who? – but he couldn't get a signal. Finally he gave up and led them off through the forest.

It was heavy going. Soon Jade began to feel desperately tired. The snowshoes felt like lead and the snow like wet cement. She kept tripping over and sprawling headlong. She wanted to just lie there and go to sleep.

Kobal produced a small metal flask and held it up to her mouth.

'Sip,' he said.

Foolishly she thought it was tea.

'What *was* that?' she said when she could speak. It felt like acid burning its way down her chest and into her stomach.

'Vodka,' he said. 'Electric soup.'

Another first.

But it got her on her feet again.

After about an hour they came out on to a winding trail through the forest – a ski trail, Kobal said – and the going was a little easier.

'Not far now,' he urged her.

She knew he was lying. It would take them days to cover eighty miles at this rate. But then after another half-hour or so they emerged into a small clearing with two strange objects in the middle. One was like a wigwam and the other like a tree hut, except that it was on top of a pole.

'We'll stop here for a few hours' rest,' Kobal said, 'and have something to eat.'

'What *is* this?' she asked him.

'A refuge – for people caught out in the snow. The tent is called a *karta*. The other's for storing food. So the animals can't get at it.'

Barmella was already pulling at the leather thongs that tied up the tent flap and Jade followed her in. It was quite roomy inside. You could have fitted ten people in without feeling it was a crowd. There was a wide bench running round the edge covered with animal skins and a stone fireplace in the centre already laid with kindling and logs and with a black metal tripod over it.

Barmella soon had a fire going and Jade watched the smoke rising up to a small hole in the roof.

'Who put this up?' she asked in wonderment.

'The *Sami*, most likely,' said Kobal, coming in with his arms full of tins.

This meant nothing to Jade but it seemed to be the only explanation she was going to get. Barmella opened a couple of tins of stew and heated them up in a black cauldron hung up on the tripod.

Jade didn't think she'd ever tasted anything so good. But she could hardly keep her eyes open. She felt more tired than she had ever felt in her life. Kobal finally took the plate out of her hands and laid her down on the bench with a pillow under her head and tucked a blanket around her. She was asleep within seconds.

It was still dark when she awoke and for a moment she didn't know where she was. Then she rolled over and saw Kobal raking at the ashes of the dying fire.

'Morning,' he said, without turning his head.

Jade just groaned. She was stiff all over. Her watch told her it was just after nine o'clock. She'd slept for about twelve hours. Barmella came in through the flap of the tent carrying a saucepan filled with snow. She hooked it on the tripod to make coffee.

Kobal had been trying his phone but he still couldn't get a signal.

'I'm afraid we're going to have to go on a bit further,' he said.

Jade groaned again.

But at least it had stopped snowing and when they emerged from the *karta* there was a pale light in the sky.

'It doesn't get much brighter this time of the year,' said Kobal. 'Not in the Arctic Circle.'

It was the first time Jade had realized they were in the Arctic Circle. And there were more firsts to come.

After they'd been trudging through the snow for about an hour they came to another frozen lake and on the far shore they could see some animals grazing – apparently on bales of hay.

Kobal made them wait in among the trees while he took a closer look. When he came back he said to Barmella: 'It's a reindeer farm but there's no one there. I've found us a couple of sleds.'

Jade had never seen reindeer before, not in the flesh. They were about the same size as the fallow deer on Richmond Park but seemed to be a lot tamer. Two of the females had been hitched up to a pair of wooden sleds, ornately carved and brightly painted, with dozens of tiny bells attached to the harness.

'Who do they belong to?' she asked suspiciously.

'Father Christmas,' said Kobal. 'Get in.'

But she'd had enough of being fobbed off.

'No,' she said, folding her arms. 'Not until you tell me where we're going.'

He stared down at the snow at his feet and seemed to be counting to ten. But then he looked up at her and said very patiently, as if to a child: 'We're going a little further through the forest until I can get a signal on my mobile. Then we'll wait until our friends come to pick us up. Is that all right with you?'

She pointed accusingly at the reindeer. 'They're not yours, are they?' she said. 'You're stealing them.'

He shook his head as if she was an idiot and started to climb into one of the sleds.

'Just put her in,' he said over his shoulder.

But Barmella opted for a more conciliatory approach.

'They belong to *Sami*,' she said. 'And when we finish with them we'll send them back.'

Jade reluctantly climbed into the second sled. She didn't have much choice.

'Who are the *Sami* when they're about?' she asked when Barmella had climbed in after her.

'The people who live in forest and keep reindeer. You want drive?'

She handed Jade the rope and told her to shake it to make the reindeer go faster and pull it to the right to make it stop. After a while Jade forgot how angry and scared she was and almost began to enjoy herself. It was quite idyllic driving through the forest, with the soothing jingle of the bells and the fir trees shedding a gentle spray of snow on them as they passed by.

After a couple of hours they stopped to eat and

Kobal finally got a signal on his mobile.

'They're coming to get us,' he told Barmella.

Who were *they*?

She tried asking Barmella when they set off again but she just said, 'Friends'. Clearly her new-found amiability did not extend to telling Jade what was going on.

It was almost dark again. The 'day' had lasted approximately three hours. Then they reached another lake. Long and narrow with the forest rising steeply on each side . . . but at the far end there was a road.

Kobal left his sled for a moment and came back to talk to them.

'This is it,' he told Barmella. 'Keep into the edge of the lake, near the trees.'

But then the reindeer suddenly started to play up, snorting and shaking their heads violently from side and side, their eyes rolling madly . . . and from deep within the forest they heard the barking of dogs.

Kobal ran back but before he could reach it the reindeer had bolted, dragging the empty sled behind it across the ice. He jumped in with Barmella and Jade and they set off in pursuit. At least, that's what

Jade thought they were doing but it soon became clear they were being pursued themselves.

Suddenly the lake seemed to be full of dogs. They burst clear of the trees on all sides and came rushing towards them across the ice, barking and yelping, each with a bearded driver on a sled behind them shouting instructions.

Kobal was standing up and urging the reindeer on and they fairly skimmed over the ice in the wake of the runaway. Jade snatched a glance behind them. There must have been at least a dozen dog sleds out on the ice, the nearest only a couple of hundred metres behind and steadily gaining. Two or three were running parallel about the same distance away and as she looked they pulled ahead and swerved in to cut them off.

Then a shot rang out and Kobal hauled on the rope until the reindeer came to a halt, snorting and pawing at the snow.

The dog sleds also halted, in a circle around them. And with a shock Jade saw the drivers were all armed with rifles.

'Who are they?' she said. 'What do they want?'

Clearly they were not the 'friends' Kobal was expecting.

'I guess they're *Sami*,' he said, cool as ever, 'and they want their reindeer back.'

But then he looked over towards the far end of the lake, beyond the cordon of sleds. Jade followed the direction of his gaze and saw a truck turn off the road and head towards them across the ice. A black truck with headlights glaring and a snowplough on the front, sending a plume of snow to either side like a speedboat – or a destroyer.

'But then again,' said Kobal softly, 'maybe not.'

27

The Battle on the Ice

The snowplough stopped among the cordon of dog sleds. A man climbed out and after looking at them for a moment started across the ice towards them.

Kobal had a strange smile on his face. He murmured something under his breath and then jumped down into the snow and walked out to meet him.

Jade looked questioningly at Barmella but her face was expressionless.

Were they going to fight?

But no, they just talked. A couple of times they looked back in her direction and she gathered they were talking about her. Then Kobal came back to the sled.

'Who is he?' Jade said, 'and what does he want?'

'His name is Benedict,' said Kobal, 'and he wants you.'

'Well, let me go to him then.' She wasn't being brave. She thought that he was a police officer or an official of some sort come to take her back to England.

But Kobal was shaking his head.

'I can't do that,' he said.

'Why not?'

'Because he'll kill you.'

He spoke so casually and yet with total conviction She felt as if he'd punched her in the stomach.

'He's the one who was trying to kill you in England,' he said.

'But why . . . ?'

He just looked at her.

'Because of what I am?' she said in a small voice.

But then she started to feel angry. She stood up in the sled and stared across the lake towards the figure walking back towards the truck. It had worked with Miss Simpson; it could work with him.

Kobal pulled her down and kept his hand on her shoulder.

'No,' he said, shaking his head and still smiling 'Don't even think about it. He's too strong for you.'

She turned away biting her lip.

'It's all right,' he said. 'I won't let him take you.'

'How can you stop him?' she muttered dully. 'They've got guns.'

'True – but we've got something else.'

What did he mean?

'Terror.' He gazed out across the ice towards the cordon of dog sleds and the drivers with their guns. 'Their worst fears. Their worst nightmares.'

'But you said . . .'

'Not him. But the others . . . they're a different matter. The only problem is – if he blocks us.'

He looked at her thoughtfully.

'It's a bit soon but I guess we haven't got much choice, have we?'

What was he talking about?

'OK,' he said. 'I'll tell you a story.'

But it wasn't really a story; it was more a list of names.

'The *Sami* have many gods,' he said, 'and many demons. There is Kalma, the goddess of death and decay, whose name means the stench of rotting corpses. And there is Kipu Tyho, the Pain Girl, who sings you to your final sleep. And Antero-Vipunen, the earth giant who sleeps beneath the leaves and soil

of the forest and absorbs the secrets of nature. And
Ajatar, the evil spirit of the forest, mother of the Devil
who looks like a dragon and suckles snakes and
demons at her breast and . . . well, many others, but
they'll do for a start. And we're going to conjure them
up, you and I, for our friends out there on the lake.'

'*Conjure them*? What – like witches?'

'Not quite like witches. More like what you did
with your teacher,' he said.

She stared at him. *How could he know about that?*

'What did I do to my teacher?'

'You saw deep into her soul,' he said. 'And you saw
something there. Her worst nightmare. And you
made it real. Real to her, at any rate. That's the power
you have, Jade, your particular talent – and now
you're going to use it.'

'But how?' she almost wailed. 'I don't know how.'

'You will,' he said.

And then he stooped down in the snow and drew
something with his gloved hand. Or rather he made
seven straight lines, like cuts, in the snow. And she saw
that they made a star. A star with seven points.

And then he took her by the shoulders and
looked hard at her and for once he seemed entirely
serious and quite frightening. And then he spoke to

her almost in a whisper: 'Thou art Astoreth, my child of the forest, and I give you the power of Beleth and of Carnivean and of Gaderel. I give you the power of Agaren and of Uzziel. I give you the power of Arakiba.'

None of these names meant a thing to Jade; she didn't feel suddenly empowered or different in any way. But then suddenly she began to feel calm. *As if she knew what she had to do.*

He stood up and became suddenly businesslike.

'Right,' he said. 'Let's do it.'

He gazed out, beyond the circle of dog sleds, to the forest and started muttering under his breath.

And then she saw something. Just on the edge of the forest, among the trees. She didn't know if it was really there or in her head. The snow was swirling around at the edge of the forest as if blown by a sudden gust of wind and she could see leaves whirling around with it and then something else, something that seemed to be rising from the ground.

She looked at the men on the lake. They were staring towards the trees as if they could see it too.

And then she felt the power. And their fear.

It was like watching a corpse climb out of its own grave. White like a tuber that has lain long underground, streaked with soil and slime and fungus. Human in shape but three or four times the size of a man with lank, grey hair down to its waist and long fingernails curving inwards and growing through the palms of its hands. Great clumps of earth were falling away from it and other things; loathsome, crawling things from deep under the surface of the earth, maggots and earthworms and slugs, dropping off the rotting flesh as it came alive, and though they were foul in themselves they were nothing to the creature they had been feeding upon. For it was the stuff of nightmares.

Then as Jade watched, it seemed to flex its fingers and the nails broke free from the flesh and it opened its mouth in what could have been a cry of pain or an enormous yawn and she smelled the stench of it which was the stench of death . . .

What was it – and where did it come from? Was it a nightmare of her own imagining or something that had lain dormant in the minds of the men in the lake? Their worst fears made real.

And it was not alone. There was something moving beside it. Something very like a lizard – a giant lizard slithering on its belly across the surface of the lake, its long tongue flickering out ahead of it.

And she knew this was Ajatar, the fell dragon . . .

But *how* did she know?

Out on the lake there was mayhem. Dogs running wild, men running after them and firing their guns into the forest or into the air, others lying in the snow and covering their heads . . .

And then the creatures began to fade. Like pictures on a TV screen when the pixels break up and they start to lose their shape.

'Hold it,' she heard Kobal calling her. 'Hold it. He's blocking us out.'

She concentrated and they began to take shape again but not as clearly as before and then she felt a terrible pain in the left side of her head that almost knocked her off her feet and the monstrous creatures began to fall apart; to shred like rags or snow sculptures, blown away by the wind.

'Fight him,' she heard Kobal's voice as if from a great distance. 'Fight *him*.'

And she screwed up her eyes against the pain and saw the figure of the man that Kobal had called Benedict standing by the truck, staring back at her across the ice.

But then it wasn't a figure – just a glare of blinding light.

And she fell to the ground crying out in an agony of pain.

When she opened her eyes it was darker and there were smaller, distant lights advancing towards her across the frozen lake. Four, five, six of them and she could hear a roaring in her ears.

Like the roaring of motorbikes.

And then she saw that they were snowmobiles. Charging in a line across the lake. Dividing on each side of the truck and coming on, roaring towards her across the snow and ice.

She looked at Kobal and to her astonishment she saw he was smiling.

Smiling in the face of death?

Then she looked back at the snowmobiles and saw it.

It had the shape of an ape, hunched over the handlebars of the snowmobile. Big, rounded shoulders and long arms and a long face hanging down low, like the face of a horse. But no horse that Jade had ever seen had eyes or teeth like that. A baboon perhaps. A baboon with a black hole for a mouth, drawn back from its sharp yellow teeth. And it was coming straight at her.

She screamed and ran.

But before she had taken more than a few steps she felt a strong hand gripping her by the shoulder and she screamed again and twisted round, lashing out with her fists . . .

But then she saw that it was Kobal and he was laughing.

Laughing.

And he said: 'It's OK, Jade, it's OK. they're my people, come to get us.'

And then he picked her up and held her out and the snowmobiles were all round them, turning in circles with revving engines, kicking up a huge spray of snow with their hunched, dark riders sitting astride the saddles like Hell's Angels − the *real* Hell's Angels − and he placed her on the back of one of them.

And the figure in front turned round and grinned at her and she nearly fainted.

Because it had the face of a bear.

And then they were off, speeding across the frozen lake, towards the forest.

28

Bleak House

London. A week before Christmas and the shop lights on all through the day because of the fog. A ghost of the fog it once was – in the days of Dickens and coal fires and gas lamps – but doing its best to remind people of the good/bad old days, all the same. Dimming the Christmas lights in Regent Street and breathing its clammy breath on the shop windows. Teasing the lions in Trafalgar Square and swarming up Nelson's Column to blind his other eye. Lurking on street corners and skulking in alleys. Creeping out over the lake on St James's Park to scare the pelican and dogging the heels of the Horse Guards on Rotten Row. A London fog with all the sneaking, snooping mischief of a street urchin. An

Artful Dodger of fogs.

Emily saw it scuttling from the headlights of a bus as she emerged from the Underground on her way to the Ministry and she stopped dead, struck by a sudden sharp memory.

There had been a fog like this the first time she had taken Jade into town, when she was a little girl of four, all wrapped up for winter. She had asked what fog was – was it smoke? And Emily had explained that no, it wasn't; actually it was water – tiny droplets of water. And the child had looked at her with incredulity . . . and something else too, a knowingness, as if Emily might like to believe that but she knew better.

They had been on their way to see Father Christmas at Selfridges.

And suddenly Emily burst into tears.

She stood outside the House of Commons with Big Ben tolling the hour and the traffic toiling its way round Parliament Square and quietly wept.

She didn't know how long she stood there. Long enough to risk arriving late for her meeting, which would have been unheard of and cause people to say she was cracking up. (Emily was always on time and usually one step ahead of it.) But eventually she pulled herself together and took a mirror and a packet of tissues out of her handbag, blew her nose and wiped off her eye make-up where it had smudged.

She had been holding herself together for so long. It was typical that it should hit her now on her first day back at the office – and over such a little thing as a memory: a trip to town to see Father Christmas.

She put her mirror away, gave a final sniff and continued on her way to the tall building in Allsham Street which the government insisted on calling the Help Office but which Emily and a fair number of her colleagues called Bleak House.

There were three of them on the tribunal. All men. One lord, one knight and one commoner – and even he had the Order of the British Empire. The chairman was called Lord Neville-Tythe of Kettering but Emily's private name for him was Lord Never-Tired of Wittering. He began the proceedings by giving his usual stern reminder about the proceedings being covered by the Official Secrets Act and warning Emily that if she as much as breathed a word to the media she would be hanged, drawn and quartered and her head set up on a spike above London Bridge.

Or words to that effect.

And then he delivered the verdict.

It was the considered view of the tribunal that 'the birth' should never have been allowed to happen but that once it had, 'the child' should have been held in a 'secure environment' while tests were carried out to establish what, if any, 'exceptional characteristics' she possessed.

Her current whereabouts was a matter for the police but if she were to be found alive . . . A significant pause during which it was possible to draw the conclusion that Lord Wittering would prefer this not to be the case . . . she was to be returned to the custody of Her Majesty's Government and held in isolation until a decision could be made regarding her future.

As for the 'special facility' at Houndwood Hospital – his lip curled with distaste – it was to be closed forthwith and its director, Dr Emily Mortlake, given an official reprimand and transferred to other duties.

When he had finished, Lord Wittering asked Emily if she had anything to say.

'Yes,' said Emily.

All three men glared at her with indignation. This was not the right answer. The right answer was 'No, thank you, my Lord, but thank you very much for asking, my Lord', after which she should have backed out of the room, bowing low to the ground, never to be seen again.

'From the moment Jade was born . . .' Emily tried to keep her voice steady . . . 'I have believed she should be treated exactly like any normal child and not as the product of some loathsome experiment. I do not for one moment regret that decision. All I regret is not taking sufficient care to ensure her safety when I knew it to be at risk.'

There was a silence during which you could have heard a clock tick – except that Big Ben chose that moment to boom out the hour. Four o'clock.

'Is that all?' enquired Lord Wittering coldly, when Big Ben had finished.

Emily could think of a lot more to say but it would have been pointless. So she bit her lip and nodded, and Lord Wittering said, 'Then good day to you, madam,' and Emily left the room in a silent fury.

One day, she promised herself, she would have her revenge. But first she had to find Jade and the truth was she did not know the first place to look.

29

The Watchers

The long winter night had descended over Lapland. The sun had retreated far to the south, leaving the northern tip of the world in darkness. A total darkness that would last for several months, through the midwinter solstice and the festivities of Christmas and the New Year and the long, dreary weeks of January and February. Several months of darkness and cold and wind and snow.

It had been snowing steadily for three days now and in the last few hours a wind had come roaring in from Russia like a pack of wolves, hurtling itself at the houses of the village and huffing and puffing at the doors and howling down the chimneys and hurling snow at the shuttered windows and generally making a nuisance of itself.

But the *Sami* had endured much worse than this and to the wind's annoyance no one took much notice of it.

The reindeer were shut up in the barns with plenty of hay and straw, the children were tucked up in their beds and the men and women were doing whatever men and women do when the long winter night stretches before them, which was mostly nothing very much.

In one of the houses, at the very edge of the forest, three men were drinking mulled cider.

They were the shaman, Jussa Proksi, and the priest, Father Johann, and the monk, Brother Benedict.

It was cloudberry cider, made from berries the shaman's niece had picked two summers ago, and the shaman poured it from an earthenware jug into earthenware bowls made by his sister on the potter's wheel in one of the sheds on her farm.

She was the same sister whose husband and son had vanished in the forest at the very start of winter and had not been seen since – though there were some who claimed to have seen them on the snowmobiles during the battle on the frozen lake. Fighting for the enemy.

For a little while the three men drank their hot spiced cider in silence as the wind banged at the shutters and blew down the chimney. Then the priest said: 'So when do you go back to Rome?'

'Tomorrow afternoon,' said Brother Benedict. 'If I can make it to the airport.'

'What do you think they will say?' asked the shaman.

'That depends on what I tell them,' said the monk.

'Well, I think we should tell the police,' said the priest firmly.

'What about?' Benedict asked him. 'The battle on the lake? No one was hurt. Not physically, at least. You could say they ran from their own shadows – or their own fears.'

The priest frowned.

'There is the small matter of the child,' he said. 'For her sake alone we should alert the authorities.'

'What authorities? No one seems to know if the castle is in Russia or Finland. It would take months to get the police to move against him. And by then he will have gone, taking the child with him.'

'So what *are* we to do?' enquired the shaman quietly.

'Watch,' said Benedict. 'Watch and wait. Don't take

any risks you don't have to, but watch everything that happens on that end of the lake — everything that comes and goes — and let me know about it.'

'We will,' the shaman promised him, as he reached for the jug of cider. 'And this time I will pick men who will not run from shadows.'

30

The Fairy-tale Princess

Jade stood on the battlements of the castle in the overhang of one of the turrets and gazed out over the frozen waters of the lake. The ice was covered with snow and the wind had whipped it into the shape of waves that seemed to come rushing towards her only to break against the rocks at the foot of the castle walls, as if they had been frozen by the spell of a snow witch.

It was snowing now. The fir trees that surrounded the lake were heavy with the weight of it and the wind was constantly dusting them down to make room for more. It was midday and although there was no sun, the sky was filled with a cold, almost electric-blue light and the trees on the shore of the lake cast faint purple shadows on the snow.

Jade wore a long red cloak lined with something that looked and felt like ermine but wasn't. Dr Kobal – the man she could not quite think of as her father – would never use the fur of real animals, he had assured her, even mink. And to further protect her from the elements – and anything else for that matter – a large brown bear stood behind her holding a red umbrella.

The bear was having some difficulty with it because of the wind. He kept angling it this way and that, tutting fussily to himself when he didn't get it right and a snowflake landed on Jade's nose or cheeks.

He wasn't a real bear, though he looked like one; he had been made in her father's laboratory in the basement of the castle deep below the surface of the lake and he had a computer for a brain. His name was Lours, taken from the French for bear, but Jade called him Laurie. He was the bear who had rescued her on the snowmobile during the battle with the hunters.

He was her personal bodyguard, her father had said, and he would guard her with his life. That was what he was programmed to do.

Distantly, from somewhere high on the fell above the lake, Jade heard the howling of wolves and the bear looked up and growled softly in reply.

There were many wolves in the forest, Kobal had warned her, some of which were friendly and some not. And other creatures that could be dangerous such as the wild cat and the lynx and the brown bear and the wolverine, which was a kind of giant weasel, also called the gulo gulo, or glutton.

And men – who were the most dangerous of all and who would kill her if they caught her.

Jade was thinking about this now. It made her more sad than scared. It made her feel she was abnormal. Unnatural. A product of her father's laboratory. Like Laurie.

People will always destroy what they do not understand, he had told her, even if it is their only hope of salvation.

Jade suddenly shuddered, but not because of the cold.

'Let's go inside,' she said to Laurie, and he shambled ahead of her to tug open the heavy iron-studded door and close the umbrella before they went down the stone spiral staircase of the turret. But the bear's great paws were not designed for closing umbrellas and he could not quite master the catch that released the spokes. After struggling with it for a few moments he made a sound deep in his throat, between a growl and a moan.

Somewhere, deep in Jade's mind, a memory stirred – a moment of what people call *déjà-vu* – *this has happened before* – and she reached out and did it for him. He looked a bit crestfallen until he saw her smiling at him, and then he ducked his head and seemed to grin back at her. He hung the umbrella neatly over one arm and stepped aside for her to enter the castle.

Jade had to hitch up the hem of her cloak as she descended the stairs and this made her feel strangely grown up and graceful – like a princess. The princess of Castle Piru.

Or the prisoner.

She wasn't sure which.

She was treated like a princess but there was no question of her leaving without her father's permission. And no chance of escaping.

Not that she seriously considered it, now that she knew what the world thought of her and what it would do to her if it had her in its power.

The short flight of stairs led to Jade's bedroom. This was a fairly large room, about eight metres in one direction and ten in the other – Jade had paced it out – with windows that opened on to the lake but were about thirty metres above it with a sheer drop. There was a large four-poster bed with beautifully carved bedposts and a feather duvet covered with an embroidered quilt. The stone walls were hung with richly worked tapestries showing hunting scenes. But the most noticeable feature of the room was the extraordinary number of mobiles that hung from the ceiling and turned slowly in the faintest of draughts. They represented different types of winged creature or flying machine and, though they appeared to be made of plastic, if you flicked one of them with a finger it would come alive and start flying around the room, until you whistled and then it would go back to hanging from the ceiling.

There were butterflies and birds and bats and hot-air balloons and old-fashioned biplanes and eagles and swans and even little dragons with wings. Sometimes, just for the hell of it, Jade would flick all the mobiles at the same time and send all the creatures flying around the room together, darting and diving and soaring and swooping, all at different speeds and in their own distinctive ways but incredibly never crashing into each other or anything else in the room. After watching them for a while, lying flat on the bed, Jade would let out an ear-piercing whistle and in the blink of an eye they would all resume their paces hanging from the ceiling as if they had never moved.

But the really strange – and disturbing – thing about them was that when she wasn't watching them flying around the room, Jade had the distinct impression that they were all watching her.

She had that impression now as she walked through the room, shaking off the small dusting of snow that had collected on her shoulders, and passing through into the dressing room beyond.

This was no ordinary dressing room – none of the rooms in Castle Piru were ordinary – for as well as Jade's own clothes it contained rail upon rail of costumes; costumes from many periods of history and many different countries. On the racks below were as many pairs of shoes and on the shelves above hundreds of hats. It was like the wardrobe department of a theatre or a film set. You could spend months, even years, here, trying everything on and looking at yourself in the mirrors standing against the walls.

But so far, apart from the cloak, Jade had only worn clothes from her own time. She felt she needed to, or she would lost her identity completely and would just become some creature of fantasy, like most of the other creatures in Castle Piru.

Jade walked on, the bear shambling behind her, and into the playroom. This was about ten times the size of her bedroom, stretching from one side of the castle to the other, and entirely filled from wall to wall with toys. So many toys it would take a catalogue to describe them but the most obvious were:

A fairground carousel with horses, lions, tigers and giant birds.

An electric train set with ten different trains that ran around the walls and across the floor in a model landscape that resembled Switzerland.

A castle filled with knights in armour and a besieging army equipped with catapults and giant bows and siege towers and battering rams.

A doll's house that resembled an eighteenth-century French chateau set in its own grounds and with dolls dressed in the fashions of the period.

A model guillotine of the time of the French Revolution.

An American farm of the early nineteenth century.

An English riding school.

A US cavalry fort, a wagon train and a Native American village.

A model zoo and a circus.

And a huge collection of amazingly realistic toy animals ranging from your common or garden teddy bear to a fully grown rhinoceros.

Many of the toys could be activated by small hidden switches or audio devices that responded to a command word and then they behaved pretty much like the real thing, except that most of the time they could be relied upon to play any game you wanted them to play.

They had been made specially for Jade, Kobal had told her — and her half-brothers and -sisters, when they arrived. But she suspected he had really designed them for himself. Certainly he was the only one she ever saw playing with them and he seemed vaguely disgruntled that Jade didn't seem to show much interest herself.

Beyond the toy room was the gymnasium — equipped with exercise machines and weights and things that looked like they were designed for torturing people but which Sophie Baer-Mellor, who was in charge, said were for developing particular muscles and which Jade was too young to use just yet.

When Jade came in she was hanging from a steel bar in a black leotard doing chin-ups and counting in German but when she saw Jade she changed to English and grunted: 'Twenty-six, twenty-seven . . . good morning, Jade . . . twenty-eight, twenty-nine . . .'

And Jade said, 'Good morning, Bar . . . Sophie,' and walked on, through another door and down another spiral staircase into the library which was filled with thousands of books and DVDs and audio tapes.

Here, too, was Jade's desk with a computer linked to the Internet, and a TV screen that covered half the wall and quadraphonic speakers so she could watch all the films and TV programmes she wanted to see and listen to all the music she wanted to hear.

The only thing she couldn't do was phone anyone up or contact them by email.

Her father said he had to put in some special device so no one would be able to trace her back to the castle but that he hadn't got around to it yet. As soon as he did, he said, she would be able to contact her foster parents to assure them she was all right.

In the meantime, he said, he had left a message for them on their voicemail assuring them that she was alive and well and would be in touch with them shortly.

But Jade didn't know whether to believe him or not.

She couldn't make up her mind what to believe about her father, Dr Kobal.

He was far too strange for her to figure out in the few weeks she had lived with him. On the one hand he had saved her life – and was still protecting her from the people who were trying to kill her. On the other . . . well, she knew he was quite prepared to tell her lies and even knock her out with drugs if it suited his purpose.

And that was the big question in her mind. What *was* his purpose?

So far – for the three or four weeks she had been here – she had done nothing but read books and watch movies and listen to music.

And 'The worst thing that can ever happen to you, my girl, is to get everything you ever wanted.'

Jade hadn't believed it at the time but now . . .

She sighed and walked on, through the study, and down another set of stairs and into the Great Hall.

This was the biggest room of all with a high ceiling and tall, narrow windows that looked out over the lake (although a cunningly angled system of slats and shutters stopped anyone from looking in, or even seeing them from outside), a great stone fireplace with massive chairs and sofas grouped around it and a long banqueting table with chairs for about a hundred people. It was where Jade dined every lunchtime and every evening with her father and where she usually found him when he wasn't working in his laboratory.

And this was where she found him now, sitting on the floor next to the roaring log fire, playing with a kitten.

He was dressed today as a Turkish sultan, in a long purple kaftan with embroidered slippers that curled at the ends. His long hair was wrapped up in a red turban and he hadn't shaved so the lower part of his face was covered in dark, designer stubble.

He had many costumes and he loved dressing up. Sometimes he dressed as an English gentleman in what he called plus fours, a tweed suit with knee-length trousers, or breeches, and long grey socks. Or he would dress for dinner in what he called the Full Monty – black dinner suit, white shirt and black tie – or in the dress uniform of an officer in the army or navy. Other times, particularly when he went out on to the battlements, he dressed as a Russian prince in a long embroidered coat with Cossack boots and hat. And two or three times she had run into him dressed as a monk in a long black habit with a cowl pulled low over his face. (This was the most alarming, particularly if you bumped into him on one of the winding staircases in the dark.) But his favourite costumes tended to be long, loosely fitting robes – either Chinese, Indian or Turkish.

He seemed to dress according to his mood, or whatever grand design occupied his mind at the time. He was like a little boy, Jade thought, or the Little Prince in a book she had read by Antoine Saint-Exupéry, who lived on his own little planet but cruised the universe on important business.

She still couldn't believe he was her father. Because whatever clothes he wore he never looked much more than twenty-five.

'Wotcha, princess,' he called to her as she entered the room. He had taken to greeting her sometimes in what he imagined to be a Cockney accent. 'Wotcha bin up to then?'

'Nothing much,' she said moodily. 'Just looking out over the lake.'

He regarded her thoughtfully, with his head on

one side and an enquiring frown on his face.

'What's up then?' he said. 'Bored?'

'A bit,' she said, pulling a face but not really thinking about it.

It was a mistake. She realized later that the worst thing you could say to her father was that you were bored.

He stood up.

'Well, we can't have that, can we?' he said. 'We'll have to see what we can do about that.'

'I didn't mean . . .' she began.

But it was too late.

He tossed the kitten casually on to the fire.

'No!' Jade screamed and darted forward but it was too late. Its fur was burning away merrily and it was letting out little squeaking noises.

'It's OK,' said Dr Kobal, dusting his hands, 'it can't feel a thing.'

'But why did you do it?' said Jade, still watching in horror as the kitten burned.

'I was bored,' he said, raising his eyebrows in mild surprise. 'I'll have to make another one that's a bit more interesting.'

'Would you do that to Laurie,' she demanded angrily, 'if *he* bored you?'

Or me?

'Hell, no,' he said. 'Can you imagine the smell? Besides, Laurie doesn't bore me, do you old feller?'

Laurie growled softly in reply but he seemed to be watching the bundle of fur burning on the fire with stupefied fascination.

Kobal crossed the room to his desk by the window and came back with something that looked like a motorbike helmet – black with a dark perspex visor.

'Put that on,' he said.

'What is it?' She looked at it suspiciously. It seemed to have built-in headphones.

'Put it on and you'll find out.'

Cautiously she lowered it on to her head. The visor covered her eyes.

'What's it for?' she demanded. Where they going for a ride? She hoped not. Not after the last one.

'We're going to play a game,' he said. 'The game of Abaddon.'

Dimly through the tinted perspex she saw him typing something on the keyboard of his computer. And then suddenly he wasn't there any more.

And nor was the room.

31

The Game

She was standing in a forest. It wasn't night, but it wasn't daylight either. It *felt* like night but she could see quite clearly. She was in a small clearing, with three paths leading off through the trees in different directions.

'Where am I?' she said aloud.

'The Royal Forest of Windsor.' It sounded like Kobal's voice but muffled and slightly distorted, as if it came from a great distance . . . or inside her head.

The place in the forest where three tracks meet.

Rackthorne.

The place where she was born.

'The purpose of the game,' said the voice, 'is to find seven people with the skills and the will . . . and the

power to save the planet. One of them is you —
but you don't know who the others are . . . Or
where to find them. And there are others trying to
stop you. But you don't know who *they* are either.
You don't know if they are trying to help you . . . or
hinder you.'

The image panned in a swift blur from path to
path and then zoomed into a figure standing beside a
tree; a figure in a long black robe with a cowl
obscuring his features — like one of the costumes
Kobal wore while he was prowling the battlements of
Castle Piru. He beckoned to her and walked away
down the path.

Should she follow? Was that what she was
supposed to do?

There was no instruction from the voice.

She turned to look down the path directly
opposite — and there was another figure, dressed the
same way.

Or was it the same figure? He, too, beckoned her
and walked away.

She looked down the third path but there did not
seem to be anyone there.

'What am I supposed to do?' she asked aloud.
'How do I control it?'

There was no keyboard, no joystick, nothing . . .

'With your thoughts,' said the voice. '*You* are in control.'

Was that true?

What did *she* want to do?

Take the path with no one there.

And immediately she was walking down it. Or rather, the trees were moving past her, for there was no sensation of walking.

And then the forest wasn't there any more and the path was winding steeply through rocks and ahead of her, in the distance, was a range of snow-capped mountains. She could feel a flurry of wind-blown snow on her face but she did not feel cold. Then she turned a corner and found herself standing on a ridge above a valley and on the far side of the valley, almost lost in cloud, there was a building, like a castle except that it wasn't fortified. It was more like . . . a monastery.

Where? What place is this?

The voice sounded urgent, as if it wasn't just prompting her but really wanted to know?

But she didn't know? How *could* she know?

And even as she thought about it the valley disappeared in a bank of cloud and she found herself walking through a street: a very noisy, narrow, crowded street filled with people and stalls, like a market, or a bazaar. The people were dressed in drab, loose-fitting robes and many of them squatted on the ground with their goods spread around them on carpets: pots and pans made of copper and brass, small wooden tables and ornately carved cabinets, songbirds in cages, hens lying on the ground with their legs tied together and piles of stuff that looked like spices, red and orange and yellow. Above her the windows of the upper storeys projected out into the street, almost meeting the windows opposite, and high above them she could see a patch of vivid blue sky filled with kites; kites of many colours.

And then coming towards her through the crowds she saw a giant figure. Not really a giant – a man on stilts. And behind him a fantastic parade of creatures: clowns and dwarfs and acrobats and a bear on a chain and a boxing kangaroo . . .

A circus. No, a parade *advertising* the circus.

The circus is coming to town . . .

And then she saw a young girl – one of the acrobats – who seemed oddly familiar.

She tried to push through the crowd to get a better look but there were so many people, so much noise. All was clamour and colour and chaos. She was beginning to get a headache and she feared the onset of a proper migraine. She wanted peace and quiet, she wanted the comfort of her own room in . . .

In Turnham Green.

Where everything was as it should be and knew its place . . .

No. She heard the voice again. *Hold it, hold it.*

But she couldn't hold it. The picture was breaking up, like the monsters on the lake, and she was in a fog, a dense fog.

But strangely she knew where she was.

She was in London with Aunt Em.

Sure enough, there she was standing next to her at a bus stop, holding her hand. And there was a red London bus arriving with the fog swirling in its headlights and they were getting on it . . .

And she remembered.

She was four years old and they were on their way into town to see Father Christmas at Selfridges. She was sitting in the bus with Aunt Em, peering out through the fog, looking at all the lights in the shop windows, dressed up for Christmas . . . And she had such a feeling of security. Security and excitement in equal measure. Such a warm, contented feeling. A feeling of magic in the air — but magic that could never harm her.

If only she could feel that again.

If only she could still trust people now like she'd trusted them then.

And then she was no longer on the bus and Aunt Em wasn't there and she was alone, walking through the streets and they weren't friendly any more and the fog was dank and menacing and the lights were dim . . .

And there were people in the shadows. People moaning and crying and screaming and stretching out their hands to her . . . and their faces were covered in running sores.

And she knew that it was the plague, the Black Death. And this was one of her nightmares from when she was a little girl. She was back in the time of the Black Death and people were dying in their thousands and the death cart was coming round the streets with the men in hoods, ringing a bell and shouting: 'Bring out your dead.' And they carted the bodies off and dumped them in great pits because the graveyards were full to bursting and if she didn't run fast enough they would throw her in the cart with all the dead bodies and bury her in the pit . . . But no matter how fast she ran she could never get away and the death cart kept on after her . . .

But this was different from the nightmare.

Because the people were wearing modern clothes.

This was not in the distant past. This was happening now. Or in the future . . .

And then she realized she was standing in water.

She knew where she was. She was standing in the streets of London, near the Houses of Parliament but the River Thames had risen above the Embankment and flooded the city. She was staring down one of the entrances to the Underground but it was full of water and there were bodies floating there. And then one of the bodies rolled over and she saw that it was her Aunt Em . . .

She screamed and the street vanished and she was in the forest again in the middle of the clearing.

Where the three paths met . . .

Try again, the voice urged her.

But she did not want to try again. She wanted to stay where she was but the trees seemed to be moving in on her. The trees were alive and moving. And there was a great gale sweeping through the forest and they were lashing their branches at her in a frenzy and then they were burning. The whole forest was burning . . . And there were people running through the trees towards her and they were burning too. The whole world was on fire.

'No,' she whispered. 'Please no.'

And the voice said: 'Fire, flood, pestilence and . . . war.'

And then she saw the coil of snakes. Like the snakes in the pit. And beyond them, something else. Something she could only sense. Something dark and unfathomable . . . and terrible.

'What am I to do?' she whispered. 'Which way should I turn? What should I choose?'

'To save the planet,' said the voice, 'or destroy it. That is the game of Abaddon.'

Then she was staring into the face of Kobal – her father – and he was lifting the helmet from her head.

'Still bored?' he said with a dangerous smile.

'No,' she said, shuddering. 'No. Not bored at all.'

She was soaked in sweat. She swayed dizzily and he led her to a chair by the fire, sat her down and poured water from a jug.

'So now you have had a taste,' he said, 'a teaser of the game of Abaddon.'

'What is Abaddon?'

'*Who* is Abaddon,' he corrected her mildly.

'Abaddon is the Beast of the Apocalypse. The Angel of the Abyss. The destroyer. Who has in his possession the key that unlocks the bottomless pit.'

He smiled again, as if it was all a great joke, and handed her the water.

But she knew it was no joke.

'Is he real?' she whispered, still shaken by the dream, or the game, or whatever it was.

'Perhaps,' he said. 'Or perhaps it is a symbol. Of what will be. If we don't change. And then, believe me, it won't be a game.'

'"*For he will bring evil from the North and a great destruction . . . and your cities shall be laid waste without an inhabitant. And his power shall be mighty and he shall destroy the mighty and the holy ones.*"'

'Another Bible story?'

'The ultimate Bible story. So now you have heard Alpha and Omega, the beginning and the end.'

'What can we do?'

'Make the right choices.'

'You mean in the game?' He didn't answer. 'Did I make the wrong choices?'

She knew that he had been monitoring her; every move she made.

'No. Not necessarily. You just didn't see them

through. You were distracted. You looked back. That's the lesson for today; the moral of the story. It's over, the life you had. Don't look back. Move on. Never look back.'

'It's how we're going to find them, isn't it?' she said, with sudden insight. 'My brothers and sisters. Through the game.'

'I reckon,' he said. 'You almost found one of them straight away.'

'The girl! The girl in the circus.'

'That's right. But you looked back – and you lost her.'

She felt a deep sense of failure – and loss.

'If I find them,' she said, 'what then?'

'What do you mean, what then?'

She didn't really know what she meant. 'Well . . . what will we do?' she finished lamely.

'We'll be a family again,' he said. 'We'll all be together. And together – we'll conquer the world.'

'I thought we had to save it.'

He shrugged. 'Same difference.'

'Put it on again.' She reached out for the helmet. 'I want to try again.'

He shook his head. 'Not today. You need to rest, get your strength back – it takes it out of you.

It sure as hell takes it out of me.'

And he turned away from her and picked up the poker and poked at the moss that had once been the kitten.

Dismissed, Jade walked down the next flight of stairs to the floor below – the ground floor. The stairs kept going down but she was forbidden to go any further for they led to the cellars and the place Kobal called his laboratory where he kept his creatures.

The creatures she had seen on the snowmobiles and never wanted to see again.

Instead she moved towards a stout wooden door set into the outer wall. Laurie shambled ahead of her and began to fumble at the heavy iron bolt with his paw. Jade waited patiently until he managed to pull it back and haul the door open. A blast of cold air and she pulled up the hood of her cloak and stepped outside into a little garden enclosed by high stone walls.

Immediately a battery of sensor lights came on, bathing the whole area in a brilliant blue-white light. Jade paused for a moment, feeling watched by hidden eyes, and then with a small shrug she continued on her way.

Everything was covered in snow but it was so sheltered there was hardly a breath of wind and the snow hung in the branches of the shrubs like dense clumps of white blossom.

She crossed to a small ornamental pool in the centre of the garden and sat down on the low stone surround, leaning forward to brush the snow from the frozen surface and exposing her reflection in the sheen of ice. A sinister hooded figure all in red . . .

Who was she? Was she real – or a dream?

She remembered how she used to stare at her reflection in the window of her home in Turnham Green and wish she was someone else – or some*where* else: somewhere interesting, having an adventure.

Well, her wish had come true – with a vengeance.

'It's over, the life you had. Don't look back.'

Kobal was right. Her old life was based on a lie, a pretence. It was over. She had to move on.

She had found her father, her real father. He was far from perfect. Not the kind of father she might have designed for herself. If you could design fathers like some people designed babies . . . But you couldn't call him boring.

In fact it would probaby be very dangerous if you did.

Now she had to find the rest of the family. And most of all she had to find herself. She had to find who she really was.

She remembered how her other father – her *pretend* father – would read fairy tales to her when she was little and cheat her by rushing through to the end – *his* version of the end:

'*And so the fairy godmother turned into a pumpkin and Cinderella got on with the ironing. The end.*'

And half-laughing, half-indignant, Jade would shout: 'No, she didn't. No, it isn't.'

Because the best stories were the ones that didn't end – but were really a new beginning.

She stood up and brushed the snow off her cloak and walked back towards the open door of Castle Piru and Laurie the Bear shambled after her and shut it firmly behind them.

Acknowledgments

With thanks to Fifer Tierra Fischer Garbesi of San Francisco for her inspiring and original advice about Jade and life in general; to my own children Dermot and Elesa for some good lines over the years; to Billie Faricy Hyett for the doll Barmella and other insights into childhood fantasy; to Chloe Taylor Gee for helpful conversations; to the teachers and children of Belleville, Fircroft, Graveney and Crofton schools in south London for the focus groups; to all the Sami families in the Kittila and Inari areas of Lapland who housed me, fed me, found me when I got lost and taught me all I needed to know about reindeer, snow and demons; to the demon bitch Dracula for teaching me more than I wanted to know about huskies; to my wife Sharon for not interrupting me in the middle of a sentence more than necessary for the sustaining of life; and most of all to Rosemary Canter of Peters Fraser and Dunlop and Beverley Birch at Hachette for turning it all into a book.

Read on for more adventure in the next
Mysteries of the Septagram

AVATAR

Coming soon . . .

No sound, no movement. The forest silent, waiting . . . The path leading on into the distance, a distant, greenish haze . . .

And then the figure stepped out from behind the tree. It was wearing a red coat – in a shiny material like a raincoat – with a hood and black boots. But it was walking away from her down the path.

It did not beckon her, but Jade knew she was expected to follow.

She hesitated for a moment.

Who to trust? The monks – or the woman in red? She was sure it was a woman. Aunt Em – or someone else?

She didn't trust any of them. Why should she? She only trusted herself – and then not very often, not with any confidence.

The figure was still walking up the path, without a

backward glance. Soon she would be out of sight.

Little Red Riding Hood, thought Jade, scornfully.

And the scorn made her reckless.

She began to follow her down the track.

And instantly it divided again. Not once, not three times – but as if it had burst in every direction, like an explosion. A starburst.

She was in a blaze of light, a blaze of brilliant white light that forced her to shield her eyes against the glare . . . She could not longer see the figure in red but she could see a number of new paths leading off, seemingly in every direction, like blades of light – or the points of a star.

She stood, paralysed by fear and indecision, blinded by the light . . . She felt that she could not stay where she was or she would be lost, her identity burned up in the star. She hurled herself forward, shielding her face with her arms . . . running directly down one of the beams of light . . .

And then it began to change. It was still bright but not so painful, not so white. More like . . . sunshine. As if she had just stepped outside from a dark room and her eyes were still adjusting to it. She stood still and squinted into the glare . . . and slowly she began to make out shapes and colours, indistinct at first and puzzling. A brilliant blue sky with birds circling at a great height. And hills, rising all around. Small hills, more like . . . sand dunes.

But they were not made of sand.

They were made of rubbish.

Great mounds of rubbish. Waste paper and plastic bags, bottles and tin cans, rags and rotting food . . . all manner of refuse twenty or thirty metres high, as tall as a house, with a great cloud of flies and other insects buzzing and crawling all over them.

And the smell . . . She could smell it as if she was really there. An overwhelming stench of decay – and the acrid reek of burning rubbish.

And then she saw the children.

A small army of children playing in the filth.

Except that they were not playing.

They were searching through it. Searching very determinedly, with serious faces. Small brown children dressed in rags, very much like the rubbish itself. And they had black plastic bags tied around their waists for collecting things. Plastic bottles, bits of glass and clothing . . . anything that caught their eye.

And two of them were eating a pizza.

Jade screwed her face up in disgust for it was clearly a pizza they had found in the rubbish, still in its white delivery box, and they were sharing it between them and picking bits off it and eating them.

She almost cried out to them – to tell them to stop it. That it was dirty, disgusting . . . And then a shadow passed over her and a large bird dropped out of the sky and landed awkwardly between her and the two boys.

The ugliest, most revolting bird she had ever seen. A vulture.

But bigger and uglier than any vulture she had seen in wildlife films. Its plumage was black and grey and its head red and yellow with a long scrawny neck and a wrinkly red sack – its crop, Jade remembered this was called – where it digested its food.

It was after the pizza but the children weren't going to give it up so easily. They were yelling at it in a language Jade could not understand and it was screaming back at them, screaming and flapping its wings as it hopped about among the rubbish, stretching out its red-and-yellow beak and its scrawny neck . . . One of the children, the bigger of the two, had a stick and he was striking at it but not getting close enough to hit it. Then another bird dropped down . . . and another.

And then the earth began to move.

Jade felt it tremble beneath her feet and she thought it was an earthquake.

But it was the rubbish moving.

The whole tip was sliding – and Jade and the two children and the three vultures were directly in its path.

The birds took off with shrieks of alarm and the children started to run. But their feet were sinking into the rubbish, as if the ground was opening up from under them . . .

And then they were gone and the dust rose around them like a great black cloud blotting the sun.

Jade had just stood there, rooted to the spot, too shocked to run or shout or do anything. But miraculously the avalanche of filth stopped almost at her feet. She stood there for a moment in the acrid cloud of dust, coughing, almost blinded – and then she started to run. But not away. She moved without thinking, scrambling up the slope of foetid, stinking rubbish on her hands and knees, sobbing and shouting for help – though she did not know who could hear her or who could give it. When she reached the spot where – as near as she could judge – she had last seen the children she began to dig into it with her bare hands, hurling it away from her with frantic haste until a hole opened at her feet: a cone-shaped pit growing deeper and deeper . . . And then she was sliding down it and she could see one of the children below, looking back up at her with an expression of . . . what? It was more like curiosity than terror. Then she stopped thinking about it and went after him like a terrier after a rabbit . . . down, down into the tunnel of filth until the light faded and the darkness closed around her.